The Cathedral Murders

©2023, J.E. Morales

ISBN: 978-1-66789-348-8

ISBN eBook: 978-1-66789-349-5

J.E. MORALES

THE

CATHEDRAL

MURDERS

1

Lima, 1991

Isabella would never forget that cold September morning when she encountered a dying person for the first time. Her day had started early with a clinical skills session at the hospital's old amphitheater classroom, and as she walked through the medical ward, she saw the floor nurse and one of the interns attending a patient. They had just found the old man lying face down with no oxygen. He was very thin. His spine and ribs protruded against the skin. The two of them easily managed to turn him around. He was probably in his seventies and looked shockingly malnourished. He was unresponsive and didn't appear to be doing any breathing movements. The nurse placed her three middle fingers over the right side of the neck, searching for the carotid artery. No pulse.

"Call the Code Blue!" she yelled. The young intern had already started pushing on the man's chest, when a dozen nurses, residents and medical students arrived at the scene.

After several minutes of chest compressions, the patient remained pulseless.

"Look at his color!" said the most senior resident, pointing at the bluish appearance of his skin. "I think he was already dead."

Everyone appeared to agree without actually saying anything.

"Let's go ahead and give one epi and do a couple of rounds of CPR for our students to practice, and then we'll call it."

There were no objections on anybody's mind.

Isabella leant forward to start doing compressions. There were not too many opportunities to practice CPR on a real human. That's when she saw a tiny black cross painted over the right side of the chest.

2

Rome, May 1992

The church of Santa Maria della Pace is located below ground level at Villa Tevere, a five-story neo-baroque building home of the Opus Dei Headquarters in Rome. Bishop Juan Carlos Silvestri found his old friend and teacher standing in front of the tomb of the order's founder, Josemaria Escriva. Over time, this church had become Silvestri's personal Mecca of spiritual pilgrimage. It was so nice to be back in Rome, he thought. Although he had felt a strong desire to become a priest from an early age, it wasn't really until the day he met Father Josef Andriso and joined Opus Dei, when he finally knew he had found his calling in life. For good or for bad, he also knew that he was going to be part of a major event in the order's history.

"It's very nice to see you, Juan Carlos. It's been a long time."

"Father Andriso! I'm so happy to be here!" Silvestri said, unable to hide the involuntary twitching of his lower lip. He was wearing the traditional white clerical collar and all-black dress shirt and pants and had a carry-on suitcase with him.

"How was your flight?"

"Long but fortunately uneventful."

"I'm glad to hear that. I'm so sorry about the short notice. I know you have a busy schedule."

"We do have a problem on our hands that we need to deal with as soon as possible."

The old priest nodded.

Silvestri stood there for a moment looking around the chapel with a grin. "And I don't mind being back to this place. It's so wonderful. I missed it so much."

"I know, my son. Let's take your suitcase to your room and then let's go have something to eat."

"I can't wait to have an Italian espresso."

"How could I forget your love for coffee?" Father Andriso said with a smile. "Let's hurry. We have a lot to talk about."

"Are we going to meet with him?"

"Yes, the Cardinal will be waiting for us this evening."

3

Lima. June 26, 1992

The unbearable coldness inside the classroom was the only thing preventing Guillermo Arenas from falling asleep. He had stayed up most of the night on call with the surgery team, rounded on the hospital patients in the morning and, later that afternoon, taken a twenty-minute bus ride to the medical school to attend a two-hour clinical pathology session. He was happy the day was almost over.

"Hey, can you give me a ride home?" he asked his friend Mario as they were leaving the classroom.

"I'm sorry, my friend, I'm actually going to Annie's house. You know, the opposite direction."

"It's okay. Thank you anyway." Since Mario started dating this new girl, he had to take the bus home more often than he would wish. Public transportation during rush hour in Lima was not for the faint of heart. *It's gonna take me more than an hour to get home. I better go eat something before I leave.*

The school cafeteria was not particularly famous for the quality of the food but it was the only thing available close by. As he walked inside, he noticed a group of students engaged in what appeared to be an animated exchange of ideas. He recognized the tall, slender guy that was clearly in charge. His name was Carlos Salazar and he was also an intern.

"Hey Guillermo!" he waved. "Come and join us"

Guillermo grabbed his sandwich and his bottle of Inca Kola and walked towards their table with some hesitation after realizing they were all part of the school Catholic group.

"I hope I'm not interrupting."

"Oh, not at all. Have a seat. We're all tired. I thought that class was gonna last forever." Salazar's tone was welcoming.

"What are you guys doing?"

"Our group is having their quarterly meeting this Friday and we were just going over our numbers from this vaccination program that we're helping with."

"It's actually quite remarkable that you have time to do some community service. Personally, I'm too tired to do anything else."

"It's really not a big deal," Carlos said humbly.

Guillermo wasn't sure what to talk about. The students' Catholic group had a strong presence on campus, always looking to recruit new members. Although he grew up in a very Catholic home, since the moment he got into medical school the religious aspect of his life had taken a secondary role. While he was not really interested in joining, he couldn't avoid feeling somewhat guilty after learning how others could use their limited free time for the common good.

"We are starting a new hospital rotation next week. I'm ready for a change. What about you?" Guillermo tried to be friendly.

"I'll be doing surgery at Santa Maria. I heard it's not too bad. And you?"

"Internal Medicine. Also Santa Maria Hospital."

"I'll see you around, then."

Guillermo finished his sandwich quickly. "I guess I better get going, it's gonna get dark soon."

"Be safe, brother. You are welcome to join one of our group meetings at any time."

The ride home was slow and painful, as he expected. Guillermo's family had moved to the upscale district of Miraflores more than a decade ago, and by now his Dad had probably given up on the idea of ever becoming a homeowner. The rent was not cheap, but the location, however, was ideal, only a few blocks from shopping, restaurants and close to major roads.

As they were getting closer to his stop, the traffic was heavier than ever. There must've been an accident, he thought. As he finally got off the bus and walked the few blocks from Arequipa Avenue to his building, he noticed an unusual increase of activity. Some of the streets had been closed and there was a large amount of police presence. He could hear the sirens of fire trucks and ambulances not far from where he was. The air was dusty, and there was an acrid smell all around. It appeared like most pedestrians were moving in the opposite direction to him, as if they were trying to get away. *What is happening?*

Suddenly, an overwhelming feeling of fear overtook him, as he worried that something terrible could have happened to his family. He ran home as fast as he could, his heavy backpack bouncing up and down hitting his lower back. By the time he climbed the stairs up to the third floor, he was completely out of breath. His Mother opened the door. She had tears in her eyes. Inside the apartment, the living-room windows were broken. His father was picking up the small pieces of glass still on the floor. He got up and gave both a hug while saying "It's gonna be okay. We're gonna be okay."

"What the fuck happened, Dad?"

"It was an explosion, a car bomb parked outside the International Bank just a few blocks from us." The blast waves from the terrorist attempt an hour later have shattered the windows of the three- bedroom apartment. "The TV news is saying there are at least twenty people dead and many more wounded."

"The damn terrorists, right? Are they attacking private businesses and killing civilians now?"

"Yes. Shining Path."

4

July 3, 1992

Police captain Raymundo Vidal stood next to a pool of blood, examining the scene and forcing himself not to throw up, as one of the officers was filling him in with the details. Rather short and with an unimposing frame, Vidal was wearing gray dress pants and a blue jacket. The detective badge that he carried around the neck said DINCOTE. The branch of the police in charge of anti-terrorist law enforcement. He walked a few steps inside the old modest house. It was early in the morning and still dark and chilly outside in the Barrios Altos neighborhood of Lima. It has been exactly one week since the bombing of Miraflores. The preliminary report stated that the home was hosting a neighborhood barbecue to collect funds for a community project. But one of the locals, Nemesio Quilca, was known to have connections with Shining Path; in fact it was thought that this gathering was just really a front for some of the terrorist support group leaders to meet. As expected, good food, beer and music were present and people were enjoying themselves until right before midnight, when five men dressed in dark clothes, their faces covered with ski masks and armed with military-style rifles, broke into the party. They ordered the attendees to lie on the floor and then proceeded to fire at them.

"They're a bunch of fucking cowards!" the young officer said.

Vidal's expressionless face did not change. "Any survivors?"

"One totally unharmed older woman, who is the only witness we got right now, and three badly injured ones that have been taken to the hospital."

"And Nemesio Quilca? Is he dead?"

"No. He's a lucky bastard. He should be on his way to Santa Maria Hospital."

Nemesio Quilca has been shot. Captain Vidal had read his file. Very poor upbringings. His family moved to the capital from Huancavelica, a very neglected region of Peru. He was not able to finish school and had to work on the streets from an early age. He used to sell stolen auto parts in the informal market. But most recently had been approached by some of his neighbors to become a community leader. The evidence suggests he is part of the group that provides logistic support to Shining Path.

"Let's look around and see if we find any evidence of terrorist presence," he was telling his officer when a tall, dark man in an olive-green military uniform approached them.

"Vidal, what are you doing here?" The tone was not welcoming.

Vidal nodded without saying a word.

"There is no reason for the DINCOTE to be here!" Without looking upset, the man increased the volume of his voice just a notch.

"Just checking things out, Rincon. No reason to be upset," he said calmly.

"You better be careful what you get into, Vidal. The Doc is always watching!"

The young police officer waited until the military man had walked away, and then he leaned closer to Vidal and whispered, "Who was that?"

"Captain Milciades Rincon. He's with Military Intelligence. He may also be one of the Frenchies' main bosses."

"The Frenchies? You mean the death squad?"

"Yes. The paramilitary group known for taking justice in their own hands. I want you to send a man to guard Nemesio Quilca the entire time he's in the hospital. Whoever did this is probably going to come back and finish the job."

"Excuse me for asking, but do you think the Frenchies are after Quilca in retaliation for the Miraflores bombing?"

"I don't know that for sure. But if that's the case, the Frenchies may be looking for him right as we speak.

5

The man was already at home by the time his beeper went off. The voice that answered on the other line gave him specific instructions. He didn't have a lot of time. *Santa Maria Hospital.*

He studied the place for a few minutes methodically, going through the checklist in his mind. It had been a crazy night in the ER. The doctors and nurses were very busy trying to keep the other two victims alive. Nobody would pay attention to another health care worker in a white lab coat.

He grabbed the chart for bed 2 and started reading as he walked towards the patient. Nemesio Quilca was lying on a stretcher in the corner of the observation area of the trauma emergency room. He was intubated and on a mechanical ventilator. One bullet had collapsed his left lung, requiring the placement of a chest tube. Another one had almost destroyed his left leg. The ER team was waiting for the vascular surgeon to come in and take him to the operating room for emergent surgery with hopes of saving his lower extremity. Despite the intravenous pain medications, Nemesio looked miserable—restless, his forehead covered with sweat. His face twisted in a gesture of extreme discomfort. His arms and legs were pulling on the restraints.

"There is no reason for so much pain," he whispered to his ear.

Nemesio looked at him.

"It's time to rest, my brother."

Nemesio shook his head side to side with violence, his eyes wide open with fear.

The man put on his Sony Walkman headphones and pressed play. He closed his eyes and took a deep breath as he injected the lethal agent into the bloodstream.

"I am the eggman, they are the eggman, I am the walrus."

6

It had now been more than two weeks since the Miraflores bombing. Other than a couple of bad dreams, Guillermo had practically forgotten about the incident. Sometimes he felt his brain suppressed those thoughts as a mechanism of survival. Or maybe it was the lack of sleep. In any case, today was Friday and the last day of the surgical rotation. It was time to go out and have a beer with friends.

The taxi dropped him off on Bolognesi Avenue across the street from the famous bar *La Noche*. He walked down the boulevard towards the main Plaza. It was cool and humid like more winter nights in Lima, but like every weekend the bohemian district of Barranco evolved into a creature with life of its own. He decided to stop by quickly to check on what in a previous life had been his favorite bar. He stood for a moment and looked around. The place had changed its name but the eclectic punk rock scene was essentially still the same. It was crowded and loud and had an overwhelming smell of cigarettes and weed in the air. He had been part of this world before, but not anymore. A local band was playing a cover version of Concrete Blonde's "Still in Hollywood." The group had won over the crowd thanks to the frenetic energy of their charismatic lead singer, a petite and slender twenty-something girl. She had dark skin, long wavy brown hair and her face had equal features of European white, South American native and black. *A freaking ethnic mix. Just the way this country is.*

He walked for another block and entered a new trendy place named *Delirium,* and approached a table where he joined his classmates Mario and Julian. Also, with them, a female medical student he had seen on campus before.

"Hey, how are you guys doing?"

"Guillermo, this is Isabella, our student on the Peds rotation."

"Nice to meet you Isabella," he said.

She nodded and smiled shyly.

"I heard about the bombing. I'm really sorry. Are you parents doing okay?" Julian asked.

"Yeah, they're alright. Thank you for asking. Between that and surgery rotation, I feel like I really needed to get out and have a beer with you guys."

Guillermo didn't expect to see a female guest with them. As he learned afterwards, Mario and Julian had finished work late after a busy day at the pediatric hospital, and had invited Isabella to come along for a drink. Trying not to stare, Guillermo studied her for a few seconds. Her presence made him uneasy. She was a girl and this was, after all, time for the guys to get together, take a break from work and talk about guy stuff. But also, he thought, she was probably not good looking enough to be seen with in a cool place like *Delirium.* Isabella had short brown hair and no make-up on. She was wearing a black long-sleeve t-shirt, dark blue jeans and black Dr. Martens boots. She did not look...very sexy.

"How is the pediatrics world?" Guillermo asked.

"It would be much better if it wasn't for the department chief's ridiculous dress code." Mario laughed. "Seriously, we aren't allowed to wear scrubs in the wards, not even when we are on call."

A young waiter with a big smile was now standing next to their table. "Here is your order of chicken wings, fried *yuquitas* and four beers."

"Thank you for ordering, guys. I'm so hungry and thirsty," Guillermo said.

"Everything okay? You look stressed out," asked Mario, probably noticing his friend was not really engaging like usual.

"I guess I'm just worried about the current situation. I've been wondering if the Miraflores bombing is just a sign that Shining Path is closing over the city. I'm afraid we're gonna see more attacks."

Mario nodded. "I hear you. Terrorists are not only targeting government institutions now but also private citizens' businesses."

"That's part of their strategy. To create fear among the people," Julian said.

"I just hope that by the time we're done with school all this shit will be over. Otherwise we're gonna have to do the specialty residency in another country." Guillermo took a long sip and put the empty bottle on the table. "I need another one."

"I really need for things to get better here," said Julian "Surgical positions are extremely difficult to get in the United States."

Guillermo slowly realized that his friends were as worried about their future as he was. Isabella did not say much. She appeared to be paying close attention to the conversation and smiled often when they told a joke. Still it was hard to say if she was having a good time or not.

The place was getting crammed full of people and so loud that it was difficult to follow the conversation. A group of girls wearing very short miniskirts started to get off their chairs and move at the rhythm of the *merengue* music that was on. Isabella looked at them almost with disgust.

"Well, it's time for me to go, so you guys feel more free to hit on some ladies," she said,

"I wish that was true, but we're not gonna hit on anyone." Mario said. "We're a group of pathetic losers." He smiled. "Seriously!"

"Couldn't agree more," said Guillermo. He would've wanted to stay a little longer but he knew it was time to go home and get some rest. *Not a fan of this music anyway.* "Which way are you going? Do you mind giving me a ride to Arequipa Avenue?"

She smiled. "Not at all."

There was not much to talk about on their way to the parking lot. He felt slightly embarrassed for asking for a ride from this girl he had just met.

"Did you have a good time?" he asked.

"I did. It's good to go out and breathe some fresh air sometimes." She had a warm, raspy voice.

"I totally agree."

As they walked, they could hear a band playing a cover version of Nirvana's "Smells Like Teen Spirit."

"Good song," he said. She didn't reply. *Maybe she didn't hear me.*

He was surprised to see her car, a Nissan double cab pick -up truck with a defiant front grill and all-terrain tires, almost a monster truck for a city full of VW Beetles and small Japanese cars.

"I do like Nirvana" she said, as they were getting in the car. "*Nevermind* is a pretty good album. But if I have to choose from the Seattle scene, I like Pearl Jam's sound a little better." Guillermo didn't expect that type of answer. *Wow.* That was impressive. She even knew the name of Nirvana's album. Not a lot of girls know about rock music like that. She looked at him for a second with a restrained smile. He noticed her big hazel eyes. *She might be kind of cool after all.*

7

Archbishop Villena-Alarcon couldn't take it anymore and turned the TV off. He closed his eyes almost in pain. *Forgive me, Lord, but I strongly dislike this man.* He got up slowly from the recliner and stood up in silence in the middle of his bedroom.

The eight o'clock news had just shown secretly taped footage of Bishop Silvestri meeting some of the military officials in charge of the war against terrorism in Ayacucho. The news anchor had focused on Silvestri's use of profanity, but the old priest was primarily upset with his total lack of acknowledgement of human rights violations by the forces of order. He had also failed to mention a recent paramilitary intervention in a poor neighborhood north of Lima during a community barbecue that killed over twenty people, most of them likely innocent victims, all in retribution for the Miraflores bombing.

"Excuse me, Monsignor?" a young man, wearing a black soutane, opened the door carefully. "Would you like me to bring your dinner here?"

"My dear Armando. It's so nice to see you. Yes, please. Here it'll be just fine."

"Is there something wrong, Father?" he asked as he placed the silver food tray on the bedside table.

"Same old, my dear friend, same old. Our country is going through very challenging times, extreme poverty, extreme violence. The president just dissolved congress, just like a dictator would do! And now we're living in a state of emergency."

Armando looked at him, confused.

"Do you follow the news at all?" the old priest asked. He had a powerful baritone voice.

Armando hesitated for a second. "Not very much, Father."

"Well, we need to fix that. Let me wash my hands first." As he leant over the sink, Villena-Alarcon glanced at the mirror. He hated to recognize how much older he looked every day. His thinning hair and beard had quickly gone from dark brown to all white over a few years, and his blue eyes, once bright and expressive, had become sad and tired.

"First, my dear Armando, you need to understand that these are not new problems. This war against these insurgent groups has been going on for more than a decade. It is true that the Shining Path terrorists are cold-blooded murderers, but the response by our security forces has also been ruthless. The government is supporting secret paramilitary death squads. Have you heard about the Barrios Altos shooting?"

"No, Father."

"It was a damned slaughter. Please excuse my selection of words. The rumors in the street say it was carried out by those vicious Frenchies, the most active of the paramilitary groups. Who knows how many hundreds of people are disappearing without going in front of a judge first? Who knows how many of them are innocent victims?"

"What is it that the Shining Path is looking for in the end?"

"The total transformation of the Peruvian society into a communist state."

For a long second Armando could not move. "Excuse me, Monsignor?" He appeared genuinely distraught. "Are we gonna be alright?"

Villena-Alarcon took a deep breath. He has long realized that getting older was making him crabbier, with the tendency to lose his temper easily, and there was no reason to frighten this young boy. "We're going to be alright, dear Armando. We're going to be alright. You don't have to worry. I may have to do something about Father Silvestri, though." He paused for a second, and then he looked at the food, smiling " Let's see here, what do we have for dinner tonight?"

8

It was close to midnight by the time Isabella got home. It was a bit of a long drive to the suburb of La Molina. As she parked next to her Dad's car, she noticed that the living room lights were still on. She was not surprised to find her Mother still awake, reading a romance novel while waiting for her.

"Did you have a good time, Isabelita?"

"Mami, you know that you didn't have to wait for me."

"Children will never understand until they become parents themselves," she whispered.

"What did you just say?"

"Oh, I was just reading. Are you hungry? Do you want something to eat?"

"No Mami, I'm fine. Thank you."

"Are you sure? I can warm up some *estofado* in one minute."

"Seriously. I'm fine. Where is Dad?"

"He's already in bed. He had a busy day. He's really worried about his business."

"I don't get to see him very often lately."

"You both are too busy. Do you go to the hospital tomorrow?"

"Yes, it's my last weekend at the Children's Hospital."

"Those kiddos are very lucky to have you as a doctor."

"I'm not even an intern yet. Well, I'm going to bed. Good night, Mami."

"Good night, Isabelita."

"Mom?" she said while giving her a goodnight kiss on the forehead, "You know I don't like people calling me Isabelita." She tried not to sound too harsh. She knew she was not good at not hurting other people's feelings.

"Sure, Isabelita…sorry, Isabella."

9

It was one of those typical, humid and overcast days of early winter when the streets of Lima are covered by the cold drizzle that the locals called *garua*. Days in which the most melancholic souls are at risk for going into full depressive states.

Isabella stood in front of the main old building and stared for a few seconds at its magnificent architecture. Although the very first *Hospital Nacional Santa Maria* was founded in 1549, the current edifice did not open its doors until 1924. The main structure with its impressive neoclassical portico and Corinthian columns welcomes you with a breath of ancient classical history and Old World wisdom. The multiple subsidiary pavilions are connected by walkways and surrounded by charming and colorful gardens that give a sense of peace and comfort. Inside them, however, things had probably not changed much for decades.

As she walked in the medical inpatient unit, the first thing she noted were the high vaulted ceilings with the tall open windows that allowed a constant flow of fresh air. A double line of metal frame beds without walls or curtains for privacy reminded her of pictures of military hospitals from the early twentieth century. She was wearing a white lab coat on top of her usual dark clothes and was carrying a blue backpack on the right shoulder and a black fanny pack around her waist.

Guillermo looked slightly surprised when he saw the new team member standing in front of him. "Hey, Isabella! Nice to see you. I had no idea that you were gonna be the student in this rotation."

"Well, here I am," she said with a smile.

"Welcome to Santa Maria!"

"Thank you."

"Please follow me this way. Let me show you where your locker is. As your intern here, I'm supposed to give you a little orientation," he said as they walked into a small classroom. "Every unit has a classroom like this where we meet before rounds. Often the attending gives a short lecture. Some days you'll be asked to present a topic. As you probably already know, this is a great place to do your medicine rotation. You'll see common diseases like pneumonia and congestive heart failure but once in a while you'll get a real medical pearl: a case of vasculitis, a hidden malignancy, an unusual presentation of tuberculosis. By the end of this rotation you'll be able to manage everything by yourself."

Guillermo sounded excited. It was good to see how her intern looked so passionate about medicine. He had black hair and dark brown eyes and was not particularly tall or handsome but had a friendly demeanor and a reassuring gentle smile.

"That sounds really great. Do we have a resident with us?"

"Yes, his name is Hugo."

The ward medical team typically included, in order of power hierarchy: the attending physician, a resident, one intern and one or two students.

"This is your patient list," he said as he handed her a hand-written piece of paper. She quickly glanced at it. Twelve patients. Bed number, last name and diagnosis for each of them.

"You probably already know how things work here. Unfortunately, the junior intern gets to do most of the physical work."

Isabella knew well that students and interns were the cheap workforce of the hospital. There was not much auxiliary personnel in the first place. "You draw blood from your patients, you take them to X-rays. You go to the lab and get the lab people to get your results on time. The first admission of the day is yours. The second is mine, and we keep rotating like that. We don't go home until all our patients are stable."

What if one of them continues to go downhill? Would I have to stay all night?

"The ICU is always full, and most of the time we get to manage our critically ill patients right here in our medical ward. It's not unusual to have a patient in shock on intravenous vasopressors. And one more thing, I guess, consider yourself very lucky, you are one of the very few that will get to work and learn in this unit. They don't call it the "cathedral of medicine" for no reason."

The Cathedral. She had heard that name before.

"That is incredible," she said, this time unable to show a little irony, which fortunately he didn't notice. *This guy is kind of a nerd!* And that was okay. Most nerds were inoffensive creatures. The arrogant jerks were the ones she had to be aware of.

"Our lead nurse is super good," he said, pointing at an older woman with short gray hair. It was clear she was the one in charge as she was the only one not wearing the traditional white nurse's cap. "Her name is Carol, and she is a seasoned veteran. You can ask her anything you need, and she will always help you graciously." He glanced at his wristwatch, a Casio with a black resin strap, "Okay. Let's go to work now! We have rounds with Casals in two hours."

The famous Dr. Casals. I'll finally get to work with him.

The first time Isabella saw Casals was a couple of years back. He was the presenter during a clinical case conference. An attending physician is given a uniquely challenging case at least two weeks in advance. Without being aware of the final diagnosis, he discusses the case in front of a usually large audience of older physicians, younger assistant professors, residents, interns and medical students to finally come up with the most likely diagnosis. It was not completely unusual to see a very respected attending failing miserably at this test. And the crowd was always thirsty for blood. The scene reminded her of a Roman coliseum, where some doctors looked more like hopeless Christians ready to be devoured alive by hungry lions. That wasn't the case with Casals. On that occasion one of the interns presented a case of a man in his early thirties who presented to the hospital with fevers, abdominal pain and coughing up blood, a symptom called *hemoptysis*. Casals reviewed the patient's presenting symptoms and laboratory results, translating them into physio- pathologic changes, and went through a list of the possible causes, what is commonly referred as the *differential diagnosis*. Isabella was mostly impressed by how Casals was always in control of his audience and appeared to be enjoying every minute of the presentation. He explained what he thought was the most likely cause of the patient's illness. After he was finished, one of the senior residents gave the final piece of the puzzle, an autopsy finding identifying the final diagnosis of hemorrhagic dengue fever, a rare viral disease transmitted by a mosquito. Just as Dr. Casals had said a few minutes earlier.

10

"Are you pretty much used to living in Ayacucho?" the bearded priest asked as the two men strolled around the gardens of the Archdiocese.

"Absolutely, Father Pablo. It took me a little while to get used to living above two thousand meters above sea level, but it's so beautiful here. Especially this time of the year between June and August, the weather is so nice, dry and sunny, not very hot. The air is so clean and fresh. Can't ask for more," Silvestri said as he looked at the clear blue sky on top of the majestic Andes Mountains.

"I'm happy to hear that," the elder said. He was probably in his late sixties and his wrinkly tanned skin was probably a sign that he spent too many of his younger years working under the sun.

"What about you? How long have you been here?" Silvestri asked.

"It's been over ten years now."

"Would you ever go back to Spain?"

"I don't know, Juan Carlos. I certainly miss my family but I don't think I'm ever gonna be able to leave. There is so much need for spiritual guidance."

"And the people are so nice!"

"What about you? Should I even ask? I don't think you'll stay here for too long, right? You have been working really hard to go all the way to the top."

"Whatever plans the Lord has for me, I shall follow his voice."

"Do you mind if I give you a little advice?"

"Is it about what the TV news showed the other day? Of course not."

"You may not like what I'm going to say. But I'm a little older than you and I may bring some wisdom to your more youthful energetic approach. I think it's very good that you have established your position of strong support to the government and the military, but..." He paused for a second. His eyes narrowed. "You have to be careful, everybody knows there is a dirty war being played when nobody is watching, and if you never acknowledge it, the people of this place will eventually resent it. Most have lost friends and relatives to the Shining Path but also to the military forces."

Silvestri nodded. "I do understand what you're saying."

"I can also tell you with no doubts that your position isn't making the Archbishop of Lima and his group happy at all." Father Pablo stared at the mountains on the horizon for a few seconds looking for the right words. "I do believe that you have fundamental disagreements with their vision of what our church should be."

"The Archbishop and his circle, just like most of the Latin America Catholic church, have been nurtured over years by socialist ideologies like the Theology of Liberation. Ideas drawn directly from Marxism that are also the base for Shining Path philosophies of class warfare. But I do understand what you are saying, Father, and I appreciate your words. But the bottom line is, if Shining Path wins, Peru will become a communist country and there will be no more Catholic church. If you're lucky you'll be sent back to Spain and I ..." He paused for a second after he realized for the first time what would happen in that case. "I'll probably be executed in public."

11

"18-year-old young woman with dyspnea and cough for two weeks. Chest X-ray shows a right pleural effusion." Guillermo presented the case in classic fashion. He described the history of present illness, followed by exposures, recent travel history, pets, family history, and so on. Then Dr. Casals proceeded to examine the patient while the Medicine team observed. A first-year resident named Hugo had also joined them for rounds. He placed the chest X-ray film on the negatoscope—the light view box on the wall. The shadow on the right side of the chest had the typical curvature seen due to accumulation of fluid around the lung.

Casals stood in front of the group ready to challenge them. "What would be your differential diagnosis? Let's start with our new team member. Tell me, Isabella, can you group all the symptoms and findings on a differential diagnosis?"

It was going to take some time not to feel intimidated by Dr. Casals, she thought. Slightly taller than the average, he had unusually penetrating brown eyes, an angular face and perfectly trimmed goatee, and spoke slowly but with an articulate, firm voice.

"I would start our diagnostic approach from the perspective of the pleural effusion," Isabella said with a weak, shaky voice. She paused for a second to clear her throat. She could feel the blood rising in her face. "Pleural effusions can develop due to infectious and noninfectious causes. Infectious causes would include bacterial pneumonia, tuberculosis, fungal and parasitic infections. She doesn't have a fever or an elevated white blood count. So, I think that an infection would be less likely."

"If you have to choose an infection in this case, what would be the most likely?"

"That would be tuberculosis. In the case of a bacterial pneumonia, I would expect to have a more toxic-looking patient, with high temperature and elevated white blood count."

"That is correct. What about some noninfectious causes?"

"Non-infection causes would include congestive heart failure, connective tissue diseases like lupus and malignancies like lung cancer."

"Any other malignancy that could cause pleural effusion in a woman?"

"Breast cancer and metastatic ovarian cancer."

"Very good. Our patient is only eighteen. She's very young, so malignancy is less likely. What would be the first and more important diagnostic test?"

"A thoracentesis."

"Analysis of the pleural fluid, very good. And what would you be looking for?"

"I'd mostly want to see the chemistry values in order to classify the fluid as transudative or exudative. Then look at the cell count differential, gram stain and cultures in case of infection and cytology exam looking for cancer."

"What do you think the fluid is going to show?"

"I think it is going to be an exudative fluid. Meaning it's likely to be an inflammatory process, but I suspect noninfectious since the patient doesn't look septic. Being a young woman, I'm thinking this is most likely systemic lupus erythematosus."

"That would be the first choice on my list, too. Really good job, Isabella. Let's also get some blood testing: ANA and anti-double-strand DNA for lupus. Hugo, be sure Isabella gets to do the thoracentesis." Allowing students to do procedures was a way to reward good performance.

"Yes, Sir," Hugo said.

Hugo waited for Casals to leave the unit to delegate to his intern. "Guillermo please supervise your junior intern on the thoracentesis. And don't forget to get a surgery consultation for the patient with the possible bowel obstruction."

"You got it, boss." Guillermo smiled. Clearly he didn't mind the extra work.

Isabella stared at Hugo for a few seconds. He wore square-frame eyeglasses and had a bushy mustache. His lab coat sleeves rolled up to the elbows remained her of a butcher.

"I'll feel much more comfortable if Hugo is not around for the procedure."

Guillermo nodded. "No worries. He won't be. By the way, you did great in rounds."

"Thank you. I was really nervous. I felt like I was getting bombarded."

"Casals often does that on your first day. It's like a little baptism. It'll get easier as the days go by."

"Will Casals be here in the afternoon?"

"Probably not. As you may already know, the staff physicians are present for rounds in the morning but most of them attend their private practices in the afternoon. I guess hospital salaries alone aren't good enough to provide for a family. But in a way that's good for us. Once the attending leaves, the interns and residents are responsible for all the clinical decisions."

12

Guillermo had just completed his surgery rotation and was pretty familiar with the surgical ward; still he had never felt entirely comfortable there. The perfectly clean, shiny floors and the strong smell of iodine solution in the air give the place a very antiseptic feeling.

"Hey Guillermo! Nice to see you in surgery-land, brother! Are you lost?" asked Carlos Salazar, as he was undressing the abdominal wound of one of his surgical patients. "Hey Freddy, can you come and help me here, please?'

"Sure. Let me just finish this note," Freddy Revilla, the other intern on the floor, said as he wrote on the medical chart.

"What do you have here?" Guillermo asked.

"Perforated diverticulitis post colon resection, open abdominal wound."

Guillermo looked at the patient's abdomen and barely wrinkled the bridge of his nose, trying to avoid appearing disgusted. "I was looking for the surgery resident, we have a consult. A patient with abdominal distention and possible bowel obstruction."

"He's in the OR right now, but if you leave the info with me I can let him know later."

"Sounds good. How do you like this rotation so far?"

"You know what I think? I'm happy that we only have surgeries on Tuesdays and Thursdays. I'm tired of holding the retractor. Freddy, can you pass me the chlorhexidine please?"

"As you can see, this rotation is not one of the most intellectually challenging ones." Freddy said as he approached them.

"And you know what else, brother? Our attending can be a jerk sometimes. Right, Freddy?"

"Dr. La Mota obviously enjoys being in the OR. Unfortunately, he doesn't care much about the postoperative care." Freddy replied.

Guillermo smiled. "I heard he's the best example of how to be a division chief; your social connections are more important than your academic credentials."

"La Mota knows a lot of people in the president's inner circle and the rumors out there say that he's gonna be offered a high position with the government. I'm gonna clean the right side here, Mr. Salas," he said, turning his head towards the patient. "Please let me know if this hurts, okay?"

"Good for him and I hope that happens, so they can hire a different attending, with a little more interest in medical education." Freddy sounded slightly upset.

"That's okay with me. I'm not planning to be a surgeon. Now, on the bright side, I 've seen a couple of cute nurse aides working here," Carlos said with a slightly wicked smile.

Freddy shook his head. "Yeah, but I've also seen the residents flying around ready to attack their prey, so you'd better make a move quickly."

"What about you, Guillermo? Not interested in having some fun?" Carlos asked.

Guillermo hesitated for an instant. "I guess not right now. I'm very busy with our medicine rotation," he said, feeling uncomfortable.

"There is no need to feel embarrassed. Guys like us have physiological needs."

"What about women?" Freddy asked.

"That's what their period is for, right?" Carlos said.

"I've actually heard that before, but I don't think that's accurate," Guillermo said, not realizing Carlos was not being serious. He didn't say anything; instead he replied with a wink and a smile. "If you don't have fun when you are young, you may be too old the next time you are ready, right? Think about it!" Then he finished taping the gauze to hold the dressing in place. "All ready, Mister Salas!"

13

Isabella placed her left hand against the posterior chest wall of the patient and tapped over the distal portion of the fingers using the tip of her right middle finger (a technique called *percussion*) while carefully listening for the area of dullness. After cleaning the skin with iodine solution, she then put on sterile gloves and drew 3 cc of lidocaine on a syringe.

"You are going to feel a little sting. That's the anesthetic going under the skin. After that you shouldn't feel any pain. Okay?" she told the girl, who was sitting up in bed, looking at the young doctors with frightened eyes.

She glanced briefly at Guillermo, who was supervising the procedure. He nodded.

"You're gonna feel some pressure. Okay?" She then introduced the thoracentesis needle in between the fourth and the fifth ribs. The girl made a mild gesture of discomfort. Dark yellow fluid quickly filled the syringe.

"Nice job," he said. "See the fluid? It's not thick like pus. It's not infected like with *empyema*. Which is a good thing, because sometimes those cases need surgery. But it definitely looks inflammatory. Let's see what the labs show."

"Thank you for your help."

"Some of the interns and residents are going for *ceviche* at lunchtime. You should come along," Guillermo said.

"I don't know. We're pretty busy here," said Isabella while writing a note documenting the procedure. "Where are you guys going?" She was not really excited about the chances to socialize.

"To a little seafood restaurant just a block from the hospital. We call it *El hueco*. It's always a good opportunity to get to know some of the other teams. Sometimes even the attendings come. "

"All right, then. I'll go, but just for a little bit." She knew this type of gathering could potentially go on for hours.

***

El Hueco was a small, modest restaurant with just a handful of tables. Most of the customers were interns, residents and doctors from different services.

"Watch," whispered Guillermo, pointing at the Ob-Gyn group at another table. "Looks like one of the students had the chance to be first assistant in a *c-section* and now he has to pay back and buy drinks for the residents. If he behaves well, by the end of the rotation he might be given the opportunity to be the first operator. Then he'll have to take the entire team for lunch."

"That's a little unfair, right? He's the only person there without a hospital salary."

"Hey, here is our star student!" said Hugo, the Internal Medicine first-year resident referring to Isabella. "Are you guys gonna have some *ceviche?*"

"I'll have a *ceviche mixto*" said Guillermo

Isabella looked at the menu on the wall. "I'll just have an *Inka Kola* and some *yuquitas*." She just wanted to have a quick small meal and go back to the hospital as soon as possible.

"What's up, Isabella, are you on a diet?" Hugo asked.

"No. I'm just not very hungry."

"This place may look a little shady but *ceviche* here is pretty good. I'll get us some."

"No. I'm good. But thank you very much."

It wasn't the first time that she was the only female in the group. She knew guys sometimes can get uneasy about it.

"Okay, no problem," said Hugo, clearly annoyed that she had declined the offer. "But I supposed you'll have a beer with all of us."

Isabella knew that she couldn't say no. It would put her in an odd situation with a senior member of the team. Still, she always thought that drinking beer during working hours was not a wise idea. "Okay. But just a glass. I have to go back to work." *I'll have to brush my teeth again.*

"How was the thoracentesis?" Hugo asked.

"It went great. Isabella did really well. Just like a textbook,." Guillermo said.

The food came and the conversation turned away from her for a moment until Hugo insisted one more time:

"Tell me, Isabella, aren't you proud to be doing your medicine rotation at the Cathedral?

"Yes, it's really great," she said, not very excited, sipping on her soda.

The answer did not appear to satisfy the resident, who was clearly getting upset. "Do you know that Santa Maria is one of the best teaching hospitals in the country?

"Yes, I know. That's the reason this was my first choice for my clinical rotations," she said, trying to show some enthusiasm with no success.

"Hugo, can you pass me the dressing please?" said Guillermo smiling, in what it looked like an attempt to create a distraction, probably anticipating his protégé getting in trouble.

But sometimes Isabella just could not stop saying what was on her mind. "Yeah, but it's probably time for some changes."

"What do you mean by that?" Hugo's tone was distinctly irritated.

Every person at the table had stopped their little side conversations and was looking at her now. She knew at that point that she had made a mistake. But it was too late to retract herself. "Maybe it's time to rebuild part of the hospital." She made a short pause. "The old pavilions are outdated. They could either be knocked down, made into offices or classrooms, but shouldn't be used for patient care anymore. New modern wards more according to new times are needed." She stopped briefly. She tried not to sound too passionate. She knew women are called emotional in a derogatory way if they show some passion. "It's going to be the twenty-first century soon, and some of these units look more like a photograph of an old military war hospital with the beds next to each other, offering no privacy to the patients. Not to mention the increased risk for spreading of infections."

Isabella felt everyone looking at her with wide eyes probably in disbelief. They were likely thinking, how dare you make such an incendiary statement? Demolish Santa Maria Hospital! Is she out of her mind?

"I think I'm going to agree with Isabella," said Freddy Revilla, one of the interns in the surgery ward who had quietly joined the group a few minutes ago. "Our current installations are not acceptable anymore. I know we all here do the best we can taking care of patients with minimal resources, but we need to adapt to the times."

"Seriously? Do you agree with her?" asked Hugo, surprised.

"I do," Freddy said.

Isabella looked at him for a tenth of a second to say thank you with her eyes. *Time for retreat.* "I'm going to excuse myself and go back to work, I still have an H&P pending." She took advantage of the small window of opportunity to escape. *Note to myself: don't ever come again to have ceviche with these guys.*

As she was leaving, she heard Hugo saying, "You know what's her diagnosis? Severe dick deficiency," followed by a boisterous burst of laughter.

She returned to the unit mad at herself for letting her emotions get in the way. She still had the bad taste of beer in her mouth. For a second, she felt like going to the restroom to throw up. She looked at her patient list one more time. *I haven't seen bed 102 yet.*

102—Jimenez. 78 female. Lower extremity cellulitis.

An elderly lady with a sweet smile sitting upright in bed, appeared excited to see her. "Are you gonna be my doctor?"

"Yes, Mrs. Jimenez. My name is Isabella. Isabella Castle."

14

Mrs. Jimenez, a 78-year-old woman with a history of diabetes, was admitted to the medicine ward with cellulitis of the leg, an infection of the skin and the underlying soft tissues. Her husband was by her side. They were a good-hearted elderly couple that loved to talk to doctors and nurses. She was started on oxacillin, an antibiotic that effectively kills streptococcus and staphylococcus, the two most common bacteria responsible for this type of infection. But after days of treatment, she was not showing signs of improvement.

"How are you feeling today, Mrs. Jimenez?" Isabella asked.

"I'm doing very well, my dear." She smiled. Her husband, sitting in a chair at the bedside, stopped reading the newspaper and said, "You guys have such a great team!"

"The other doctor that works with you, Dr. Arenas. He's very nice, too. Is he your boss?"

"Guillermo. Yes, he's an intern." That apparently didn't mean anything to the old lady as she just stared at Isabella with a blank face. "He's in his last year of medical school," Isabella explained.

"And what about you, dear?"

"I'll be an intern next year."

Carol, the head nurse, was watching the interaction from a short distance. "She's such a sweetheart. Isn't she, Dr. Castle?"

"Yes, she is," Isabella said with a not very confident smile. "Can I talk to you for a second?" She whispered as they both walked away. Isabella looked at her closely for the first time. Carol had pale skin, delicate facial features and big black eyes, and despite being probably in her mid-sixties she was still a beautiful woman. "I'm worried about her, Carol. Her leg remains swollen and red, she still has low-grade fevers and her white blood count is still very high."

"During rounds, the team's plan was to add a second drug to broaden the antibiotic activity."

"I know, and that's okay, but what if it's something else?"

Could she have something else? Isabella was especially worried about a deep venous thrombosis—a blood clot—in the leg, since lack of mobility is a risk factor and Mrs. Jimenez had been mostly bedridden for over two weeks. Unfortunately, most public hospitals in Peru didn't have the technology needed to make the diagnosis. As with many other modern imaging exams, ultrasound Dopplers were only available in private clinics. And they usually had to be paid by the patients and their families with out-of-pocket cash.

Isabella spoke with the husband. He could pay for the test but couldn't afford the expensive hospital ambulance for the ride.

"How do you like rounding with Casals?" Guillermo interrupted her thoughts suddenly.

"Very much. He's a really good teacher."

"Let me tell you something most people don't know about him. During his college years, he had long hair and a big bushy beard. He was the Latin-American hippie of the sixties, occasional marihuana smoker."

"Ha! No way! He's so serious, I can't even imagine him like that."

"It was trendy for university students and intellectuals those days to have this idealized romantic version of socialism, the Cuban revolution and Che Guevara. Someone mentioned that he even joined a left-wing party. I guess at some point he chose science over politics and decided to apply to medical school."

"How do you know all these things?"

"Doctor Carlos Zubieta shared with us after rounds a while ago."

"I've never met Dr. Zubieta. He's the one who introduced the bedside teaching rounds the way they are now, right?"

"Correct. He trained Casals, too. I guess he represents the classic master clinician model that Casals loves. He is retired now but occasionally attends rounds."

Isabella didn't say anything. Her thoughts were already somewhere else.

"Something wrong?"

"Sorry, I'm fine," she said politely. "Hey Guillermo, I wanted to ask you something about our patient, Mrs. Jimenez."

15

"Good morning, Mr. Prime Minister," Bishop Silvestri said, holding the telephone in between his right shoulder and neck while lighting up a cigarette with his left hand.

"Father Silvestri! It's nice to hear from you!"

"I read the very sad news about Dr. Loayza in today's paper," he said as he walked back and forth around his desk in the dioceses of Ayacucho.

"Yes, very sad."

"What exactly happened?"

"A terrorist ambush. Dr. Loayza was driving back to Lima after a weekend at his beach house in Punta Hermosa when the car in front of him suddenly stopped. A young man, probably in his early twenties, came out of the car and shot the Minister in the head twice from a short distance. He died a few minutes later before the ambulance could make it to the scene."

"That is terribly sad. We really need to stop this madness."

"We received a video that we haven't made public, showing one of the terrorist leaders claiming authorship of the attack. The bastards!"

"Like I said, this madness needs to end. In any case, if the president has not chosen his next minister of health yet, if I may suggest, I think I know somebody that would be an excellent candidate for that position."

"I don't believe he has any serious candidates yet. Who do you have in mind, Father?"

"Dr. Augusto La Mota, a well-known and highly respected surgeon who also has leadership experience in healthcare administration as he's currently the director of Santa Maria Hospital."

"I know Dr. La Mota. Great guy indeed. I will definitely bring it up to the president for sure, Father."

"Thank you, Mr. Prime Minister."

16

Isabella noticed Guillermo's brown eyes narrowing down as she explained her plan "What do you think?" she asked, worried he was going to say no.

"You wanna get Mrs. Jimenez, who can barely walk, in your pickup truck and drive her to a private doctor's office to get a venous ultrasound? You can't be serious!"

"Yes, Carol already called the office and they're holding a spot for us if you agree. The husband will pay for the test—for which, by the way, Carol got them to drop the price by fifty percent."

"You've got to be crazy! What if something happens to her on the way? What if she falls and breaks her hip? What are we going to tell Casals?"

"We can tell him tomorrow once it's done."

Guillermo shook his head and looked down in disbelief. "I can't believe we're doing this."

There was no time to waste, a blood clot in the leg can break and travel through the circulation into the lung vasculature—a potentially lethal condition called pulmonary embolism. She squeezed Mr. and Mrs. Jimenez, Guillermo and a wheelchair into her truck and drove them to a well-known vascular surgeon's private practice clinic thirty minutes away.

"This is a pretty big car you have," Guillermo said as she was looking for a parking space.

"I know, the style is not very ladylike." She smiled. "My Dad got it on my twenty-fourth birthday and specifically chose a vehicle this size to protect me from the out-of-control traffic of Lima."

"I don't blame him. Driving in this city can be a dangerous adventure," he said laughing.

Once they were checked in, they all sat down around Mrs. Jimenez' wheelchair. Isabella felt the entire group was completely out of place in the swanky office's waiting area.

"How long have you guys been together for?" Guillermo asked the old couple.

"We've been married for forty-nine years," Mr. Jimenez said proudly. "But we've been together since she was twelve and I was fifteen."

"Next year we will celebrate our golden anniversary," Mrs. Jimenez added while looking at her husband in awe.

"Fifty years! Wow, that is incredible!" Guillermo said.

Isabella just sat there smiling. Sometimes she wished she was naturally more outgoing. She wanted to ask: *Do you have any advice on how to have a long, loving relationship?*

Once Mrs. Jimenez got on the exam table, the ultrasound took only a few minutes and demonstrated a blood clot extending from the veins mid-thigh to right below the knee.

"It's called a deep venous thrombosis, or DVT for short. It's a blood clot in the leg veins," Isabella explained. "If we don't treat it right away with blood-thinning medicines, the clots can break, travel with the circulation up to the chest and cause a blood clot in the lungs. A blood clot in the lung can be extremely dangerous, sometimes even fatal."

"Thank you very much, doctors. You've been really good to my wife and I. I really appreciate all that you're doing. I really do," Mr. Jimenez said with tears in his eyes.

"You don't have to thank us for anything. We're just doing our work," Guillermo said.

Once back to the hospital, Mrs. Jimenez was started on intra-venous blood thinners the same evening.

By the time Isabella got home that evening, her parents were already in bed. She was exhausted but in a way feeling accomplished, knowing the extra effort had paid off. Despite the limitations, they were able to appropriately diagnose and treat Mrs. Jimenez. She noticed that lately, her mind had been occupied with more positive thoughts rather than self-destructive ideas. She was not thinking about her ex anymore. The previous year had been a difficult one. Her brother Diego had moved away to the United States. With no close friends, she had spent her last summer off mostly by herself, in her bedroom, reading and re-exploring some old music. She stared for a few seconds at her cassette tapes and CDs: The Smiths, Joy Division and Depeche Mode. Certainly not the most uplifting music. Things have not gotten much better during the Ob Gyn rotation, which she could not have hated more. Nevertheless, Isabella had not felt content like this in a long time. It felt good to be away from the classroom setting and able to apply the basic sciences knowledge learnt through the first years in real-life cases. She was excited about the intellectual challenge of the search for the diagnosis. A good patient's outcome was the best reward. She was able to appropriately diagnose Mrs. Jimenez, and hopefully she could soon go home to be with her charming husband.

I'll bring them a present for their fiftieth anniversary.

17

Isabella knew Casals would be mad the next morning but she didn't lose much sleep about it. She had no doubts she had made the right decision. In a way she felt a little sense of accomplishment. She had broken the rules but it was for a good cause. As she drove to work that day, she couldn't wait to check on Mrs. Jimenez, hoping her leg was already showing signs of improvement. And she couldn't wait to see Mr. Jimenez' face of happiness, thinking his wife will be discharged from the hospital soon.

"Where is Mrs. Jimenez?" she asked Carol, the charge nurse, after noticing her bed was empty. "Did you move her somewhere else?"

"She died, Doctor."

"What? " For a second she thought she heard the wrong thing. She died? How is that even possible? "I don't understand. How?"

"It happened in the middle of the night. All of a sudden, she went into cardiac arrest. Probably a pulmonary embolism, I would say. Regardless of the cause they told me she passed peacefully. Thank God for that."

Mrs. Jimenez died. She stood up there in the middle of the unit unable to move. What could have happened? A pulmonary embolism makes sense, she thought; one of the blood clots in her legs traveling to the lungs. If large enough, the clot can obstruct the blood flow to the heart, causing the blood pressure to drop, in severe cases leading to a cardiac arrest. However, she had been started on intravenous blood thinners immediately after they arrived from the test.

Suddenly, with no explanation, she had the urge to see her body.

"Where is the body, Carol?"

"Excuse me doctor, what did you just say?" Carol asked, her eyes wide open in surprise.

"Her body, Carol. Mrs. Jimenez' body."

"It's probably still in the morgue, waiting for the family or the funeral home to pick it up."

Without answering, Isabella left the unit. She didn't care that she had still not seen any of her other patients. There was a strange force pulling her to see her patient one more time.

The morgue was a cold, desolate place in the lower level of the hospital. For Isabella, it felt more like a dungeon. She was familiar with the area since it's next to the pathology lab, where they used to look at slides of diseased organs under the microscope. As she approached she could feel the unmistakable smell of formaldehyde.

She opened the door with hesitancy hoping nobody was going to yell at her. Hospital workers tend to be very protective of their territory. An impressively overweight individual was sitting on a chair, leaning against the stainless steel autopsy table. He was wearing a dirty white lab coat and appeared to have fallen asleep while reading the newspaper.

"Hi," she said, "I was the intern in charge of Mrs. Jimenez. Would it be okay if I take a look at her body?"

"That's a very unusual request" he said as he slowly woke up from his state of hibernation. "Why would you wanna look at the body?"

Isabella didn't quite know what to say right away. She looked around. The room was relatively small, surrounded by old metal shelves with books and cabinets with many specimen jars.

"She was my patient for more than a week. She passed overnight. I didn't have the chance to say goodbye."

"Fine. Go ahead," said the guy while trying to remember what was the last part of the paper he read.

She uncovered the cadaver lying on the stretcher. It was her. Mrs. Jimenez' aura of kindness looked unchanged from before. Only her color was different. Something in between white, purple and gray. She grabbed her hand. It was room temperature cold. Although they had not talked as much as she would have liked to, Isabella felt they had developed a special bond. She had finally started to think that it was possible for her to empathize with people. *Maybe I have some feelings. Maybe I'm not that weird.* But at the same time, she could not stop having some sort of guilt for not being able to prevent her death.

The morgue guy did not look happy with the unexpected presence of the young doctor. Isabella caught him staring at her possibly with curiosity at the beginning but slowly she felt the sense of lust on his face was becoming too much to ignore. Clearly uncomfortable, she needed to wrap things up and go back to the unit.

Isabella explored Mrs. Jimenez' body up and down. Her leg was still swollen and the redness had more of a purplish tone now. She appeared in peace, almost smiling. *Her face...*there was something new about her face.

"Who did this to her face?"

"Excuse me?"

"Her face!"

"What are you talking about?"

"Her face. Look at it."

He let out an exasperated sigh and approached in slow motion. "What is it?"

He got closer. Now he could see it. Somebody had painted a small black cross on her left cheek.

"What is this?" she asked him again.

"I have no idea, ma'am. That's the way she came. Nobody had touched the body since she's been here. Maybe a priest said a prayer for her on the floor. I don't know."

"A prayer and face painting? Never heard of anything like that before."

The obese guy now looked clearly irritated. He had enough questions.

"You better go. I have stuff to do here. Go before I call your supervisor. "

18

Guillermo had anticipated this moment. Unfortunately, he did not foresee how bad it was going to feel.

"I can't believe what you did! Why didn't you tell me before?" Casals raised his voice. He didn't look like he was trying to hide how mad he was.

Isabella and Guillermo were standing in front of him, avoiding all eye contact.

"I'm gonna have to talk to Dr. La Mota, who is not only the director but also in charge of all the clinical rotations in the hospital, and Dr. Cazorla the Dean. I'm afraid you are gonna be in trouble, you may even get suspended. I don't know. I've never seen a situation like this before," he said, shaking his head.

"It was my idea, sir. Guillermo is completely innocent."

"Guillermo is your intern, he is your supervisor during this rotation and he's also responsible for what you do, too. If he wasn't sure about it, he should have asked Hugo, your resident."

"I thought the test was necessary to make the diagnosis, sir," she said, looking down.

"Unfortunately, this is a poor country and this is a poor hospital and our patients are also poor. There are going to be many instances where we may not be able to make the diagnosis because the test needed is not available or it's just too expensive and the patients can't afford it. It happens every day. We try to do our best with the tools that we have. What would have happened if she had an emergency while you were driving? If she became unresponsive or developed an irregular heartbeat or went into cardiac arrest? She could have died while in your car and we all would be liable for that!"

Guillermo looked at Isabella's eyes for a second. "We're very sorry, sir. This will not happen again," he said. She understood this was not the time to argue with the boss.

"Well, she died later the same night, how do we know she didn't die from a pulmonary embolism triggered by the car ride?" Hugo, who had been listening in silence, added more uncertainty.

"Long car trips are a risk factor for venous clots for sure. The car ride to the vascular office was relatively short. Although unlikely, it's certainly a possibility that we cannot disprove," Casals said as he was leaving.

Hugo waited until Casals was gone and then turned towards Guillermo. "Listen my friend, you need to keep your student under control. She doesn't tell you what to do. Okay. Start practicing now and maybe your future wife won't be the one in charge at your home."

Thank you for your invaluable input, asshole.

"Let's take a break, Isabella. Let's go have a snack."

"Okay. Cafeteria?"

"No, there's this little stand next to the surgery building where you can get soda and crackers."

"I'm sorry I got you in trouble," she said as they exited the medical ward.

It was chilly and humid outside, a reminder that some days it was better just to stay indoors during the winter months in Lima.

"I knew that wasn't the right thing to do. I should have been more careful," Guillermo said.

"But I still think that was the right thing to do. We had to be certain of the diagnosis before starting somebody on a full dose of anticoagulants."

"What if, like Hugo says, she threw a clot because of the car ride?"

"Hugo is such an asshole. I don't think so. There is something else that I haven't told you. I went to see Mrs. Jimenez' body at the morgue."

Before she could explain further, they found Carlos, sitting on a bench, smoking a cigarette right outside of the surgical building. He didn't appear to be in his usual good mood.

"What's happening? " Guillermo asked.

"You know, not even a week into this rotation and I'm getting tired of being kind to the surgery attendings and residents, who behave like jerks most of the time."

Guillermo knew that feeling. "I've been there too. I'm sorry to hear that."

"When things don't go as expected in the OR, Dr. La Mota can become the most vicious human on earth. He'll throw a surgical instrument at you if you're not careful."

"He's actually mad because this cute OR tech would not go out with him, " Freddy, his Surgery rotation partner, added with a straight face as he came up behind them.

"She's actually dating the major asshole surgery chief resident!" Carlos said.

"No surprise there. Usually the highest ranked asshole has prima nocta rights," Freddy said.

"Prima what?" asked Guillermo.

"Prima nocta was the legal right of medieval lords to have sex with a female subject on her wedding night," Isabella explained with a disgusted expression.

"That sounds repugnant. Unless you were the medieval lord, of course." It didn't take too long for Carlos to find his typical sense of humor.

"Well, I have some good news for you, Carlos," said Freddy. "Did you see who is the new head of the Ministry of Health?"

"Not really. I haven't been following the news for a long time."

"Well, it is our very beloved attending, Dr. La Mota."

"Wow, very interesting. I would imagine he won't be rounding with us anymore."

"Exactly. He will have to put his clinical practice on hold for the time being. I was told this is his last week at the hospital."

"Let's hope his replacement is a little better of a teacher."

"You know, my group is gonna be very happy with him becoming part of the government."

"Your group? Meaning the Catholic group? Why is that?" asked Guillermo, who was mostly distracted, still bothered by being scolded by Casals.

"Dr. La Mota is an Opus Dei supernumerary."

"Remind me what exactly was that?"

"Somebody from the secular society, usually a professional, you know, like a lawyer or a doctor, that is married and has a family but is very involved with the activities of the order."

"I see."

"There are some social issues that are important for the church, and La Mota as a part of the government may be able to support, for example, being sure abortion remains illegal and maybe promoting some anti-homosexuality laws. I'm tired of seeing gays everywhere."

"Anti-abortion laws that only affect poor women with no access to health care," Isabella quickly pointed out. "The rich girls will still be able to get a procedure as long as they are able to pay for it. Sounds great!" Her voice was clearly aggravated. "I'm gonna get a soda. I'll see you back at the unit, Guillermo."

"Wow, she is in a bad mood! Are you guys dating?" Carlos asked.

"No!" He was taken by surprise by the question.

"I have to say she looks kind of cute with her short hair and boyish looks, but I heard she might be a lesbian. And she drives a big pick-up truck that would destroy my VW."

"Your Beetle? The *hoochie mobile* will get totaled after crashing against your little brother's bicycle." Freddy had an ironic, interesting way to put things.

"You know, the lesbian thing makes the whole thing much more interesting," Carlos said with a little boy's naughty smile.

"Are you saying homosexuality is acceptable now? You just said you were tired of seeing gays everywhere?" Not very often did Guillermo show his disagreement.

"Not really, you know, but I'm sure the Lord can make some exceptions given the right circumstances."

"With that kind of thinking, I don't know if you're gonna go to heaven." Freddy's face was serious. Guillermo couldn't tell if he was just trying to be sarcastic or not.

"Brother, you can always repent and pray for forgiveness," Carlos smiled with a wink, like he usually did. "Let's pray for forgiveness, brother and sisters!" he said while lighting another cigarette.

"Well, I'm happy we made you laugh," Guillermo said, thinking there was something about Carlos that made him feel uneasy every time. "I think it's time for me to go back to the medical ward. Nice talking to you guys!"

19

Although talking to the surgery interns had briefly made her mad, Isabella could not stop pondering on Mrs. Jimenez' bad outcome. When she returned to the floor, she found Mrs. Carol, sitting at her desk, filling out hospital forms. Part of her usual work as the unit head nurse.

"Carol, I don't understand. She looked so good, she was getting better."

Carol stood up and walked towards Isabella with a friendly smile.

"I know, doctor, she was doing much better. She probably had a massive pulmonary embolism." Isabella knew Carol had been working at Santa Maria Hospital for over forty years now and rumor said she was getting close to retiring one of these days. She was already the unit charge nurse when Dr. Casals was an intern and had witnessed his development into an outstanding attending physician.

"You are probably right, Mrs. Carol. A major pulmonary embolism can cause sudden cardiac arrest and we knew she had a blood clot in the leg. We did start a heparin IV drip, but is not unusual for the medicine to take several hours to reach a full anticoagulant effect. So, it fits quite well." Isabella took a deep breath. She didn't want to suddenly start crying. She could not afford to look weak. "Still, I feel really bad, especially for the poor husband."

"It's okay, Dr. Castle. I imagine this is the first time this has happened to you. It's not easy to lose a patient for the first time. You did the best you could. Unfortunately, it's not always up to us. Mrs. Jimenez is in a better place now." Mrs. Carol had a soft, calming voice.

"Thank you."

Mrs. Carol turned around ready to get back to her hospital paperwork.

"I noticed something, though." Isabella shrugged her shoulders, puzzled. "I went to the morgue to see her body and I noticed a tiny black cross painted on her cheek. Do you know what that could be, or who could have done that?"

Carol's face suddenly changed. Her supportive, loving smile slowly faded. She crossed her arms and looked away, rather uncomfortable.

"I do not know, doctor. I need to get back to work. It was nice talking to you," she said as she left the unit.

20

York, England. Summer 1985

"I think you'll understand now why I've always considered York one of my favorite cities in Europe," Father Joseph Andriso said, as the two priests walked down the pathway towards the York Museum Gardens. It was nice for once to be able to mix anonymously with the other tourists as they were dressed in casual layman's clothes. After several days of nonstop rain in north England, the sun shone without restraints and the weather could not have been better to be outside.

"I can see that, Father. There's so much history to learn here," Silvestri said, grinning with joy. Over the years, Father Andriso and him have embarked on the project of visiting all the most important cathedrals in Europe. They had taken an early train from London to York on a mission to explore the magnificent cathedral commonly known as York Minster, but also to see as many historic sites as possible, including York castle, the Viking museum and walking up and down the famous old street known as the Shambles.

"But what I really wanted you to see, son, is right here!"

The two men were now standing in the center of an imposing set of white stone walls with gothic arches.

"These are the ruins of what once was a very wealthy Benedictine abbey. The glorious St. Mary's abbey. A few years after Henry VIII became the head of the Church of England, monasteries, convents and abbeys were expropriated from their original Catholic orders. "

Silvestri looked at the ruins still standing after centuries. There was a sense of calmness within its walls. "It had to be quite spectacular, Father."

"They say it was. For some, just another piece of British history. But for me, more than anything, a reminder that our church is always at risk of being attacked by multiple forces. Political ideologies, the government, other religions; however, you must never forget that the danger itself can also come from inside our own church."

"Inside our own church, Father?" Silvestri raised his eyebrows in disbelief.

"That is correct, my son. And our mission in this world is to protect our church. That is why we are here, my son. You should never forget. We must be champions of our faith. We must protect our church."

21

It took almost a week before Isabella felt confident enough to tell somebody else about her concerns.

"Are you sure?" asked Guillermo.

She noticed he was having a hard time following the narrative.

"Yes. Both patients had a small black cross painted on their bodies. The first one, an older malnourished patient, had it on the chest and the second one, Mrs. Jimenez had one on her face. Why would anybody do that?"

"Someone that has access to the bodies after they passed away probably did. Like someone that works in the hospital morgue. Maybe they are 'marked' as a part of their post-mortem process."

Isabella shook her head. "The first time I noticed it was while we were doing CPR. This was a year ago, but I still remember clearly. I was thinking what if it was left there by the person responsible for the deaths? The first guy was found lying on his belly face down on the pillow, no breathing. The nurses thought that someone had to turn him as he was too weak to do it himself. So, the whole thing was very suspicious. Ask Martin Benitez, he was the intern doing CPR. He was there."

"Did they do a post-mortem exam or was the case ever reviewed? "

"I honestly think nobody paid much attention. He was a chronically ill, poor old man. And his prognosis was probably not good regardless."

"But why would anyone want to kill a defenseless patient?"

Isabella did not have answers. She felt like her brain was foggy. Something she had never experienced before. *This is so confusing*. She looked around.

"What time is it?" She just realized she had nothing to eat all day.

"It's almost three 3 o'clock."

"I'm so hungry." *No wonder I can't think right.* "Can we take a break and go have something to eat?"

"Sounds like a good idea. I'm hungry too."

"But not to *El Hueco* again, Okay? Do you have any other secret places?"

"There is a snack kiosk in the lobby of the clinic building."

* * *

As they approached the outpatient area, Isabella was surprised to see the large number of visitors, probably waiting for their turn to be seen. "I didn't know this place was so busy!"

"Most of these people have no health insurance. The medical visit is very inexpensive, but they have to come here early to get in line and wait for several hours before they can be seen."

"Excuse me, doctor?" a middle-aged woman asked Guillermo. "Can you tell me how to get to the obstetrics pavilion?"

"I'm actually not sure. Sorry."

"It's actually on the opposite side of the hospital," said Isabella. "Just follow this pathway and the obstetrics building will be on your right."

"Thank you very much, senorita."

"Okay, let's go get a snack. I'm so hungry," Guillermo said after the lady walked away.

"Did you see that?" Isabella said, trying not to show her frustration.

"What exactly?"

"We both are wearing lab coats. We both wear our tags with our names. However, she called you doctor and then she referred to me as "señorita." It's so discouraging!"

"Why? It doesn't seem like a big deal. She was very nice and respectful."

His partner's response was another stab of disappointment that she was unfortunately too used to. Male lack of awareness appeared to be widespread. "People have difficulty seeing women as doctors. It's probably the same for any position of power like a business executive or high-rank politician. It's just a sign of how our society has been modeled by men. It's gonna take a long time before things change and nobody is surprised to see a female doctor or prime minister."

22

"Good morning gentleman, sorry I'm five minutes late," Archbishop Villena-Alarcon closed the door of the main conference room at the Archdiocese of Lima, the center of power of the Peruvian Catholic church. "I need you to tell me everything you know about Father Silvestri, all the way from the beginning. As you know, I'm getting old and my memory isn't as good anymore and sometimes I need you to repeat things to me more than once." The old priest sat back on his leather chair and scratched his shaggy white beard.

"Of course, Monsignor," said Father Pedro, one of the two priests across from the table. "Father Juan Carlos Silvestri was born in Lima. Grew up in an upper-middle-class environment. The third of four children. Parents highly educated, both were university professors. He attended an all-boys Catholic school." Father Pedro read from his notes.

"During an interview on TV he said that's where he first heard God's call for a life of service in priesthood," Father Manuel added.

"Of course he did!" said the Archbishop, rolling his eyes. "Please continue, Father Pedro."

"He was a bright student, very smart. His tremendous potential was always obvious to everybody, and he was recruited early on by Opus Dei, which..."

"Opus Dei is always trying to capture rich, intelligent kids, like..." The Archbishop did not finish the sentence. "Sorry for interrupting again. I'll keep my mouth shut now."

"Opus Dei then facilitated for him to attend the University of Navarra in Pamplona, Spain," Father Pedro continued with his presentation. "The University of Navarra was founded by Jose Maria Escriva himself."

"Jose Maria Escriva, the founder of Opus Dei," the Archbishop said. "I have a bad memory but that I remember."

"It was in this academic environment where he met Father Josef Andriso, and his real journey with Opus Dei started off. He spent some time in Rome. Father Andriso introduced him to many high-ranked officials in the Vatican. Mostly conservative figures with close ties to their order. At some point when they thought he was ready, Silvestri moved back to Peru, became a college professor in theology and eventually became the Bishop of Ayacucho."

"And that's when he started to become a pain in my ass," the old priest growled. "What do we know about this Andriso? I don't remember his name. Is he Italian?"

"His family emigrated to the United States from Czechoslovakia. Grew up poor in a working-class neighborhood in New York City. Excellent student, was able to attend Georgetown University on a scholarship where he studied theology. He is an expert in canonic law."

"Georgetown is a Jesuit university. How come he didn't stay with us?"

"At some point he joined Opus Dei. I'm not aware of how this happened, though."

"Monsignor," interrupted Father Manuel, "Andriso is considered one of the most brilliant minds inside Opus Dei. And he's Silvestri's mentor and advisor."

"So you are saying, our adversaries are extremely bright?" Villena -Alarcon shook his head with frustration. "This isn't getting any easier. Please continue."

"By the time he became bishop of Ayacucho, Shining Path's activity had already begun. Silvestri has always been very supportive of a strong military presence in the area and had avoided denouncing any human rights violations by the law forces. I'm afraid one of these days he's going to proclaim his support for the death penalty in cases of terrorism."

"The government and especially Valentin Montero's generals would love that. That's the kind of partnership they don't mind."

"I'd like to remind you that Silvestri is a very charismatic figure, and according to some recent polls his approval ratings are very high with more than seventy percent of the people agreeing with his position on terrorism," Father Manuel said.

"But most of the church leaders, including myself, believe that in the current context of unjust social structures, our priorities have to be with the poor and the most in need."

"But for some members of Opus Dei, some of those ideas like the ones from Theology of Liberation are not much different than communism."

"You are mostly right about that, Father Manuel. But for many years now the Vatican has been very welcoming of the Opus Dei conservative approach. As you know, Escriva was beatified last May and some people suggest that Pope John Paul is going to push for a quick canonization," the Archbishop said.

"What do you think they are trying to achieve?"

"I don't know for sure, gentlemen. It's possible that they want the Catholic Church ideologies to move closer to their more conservative roots."

"But as long as you are in charge, Monsignor, our church priorities in this country are going to remain the same. Our cause is devoted to the poor people of Peru," Father Pedro said.

The Archbishop did not reply. His blue eyes were staring at the painting of Saint Agustin on the wall across the boardroom. *As long as I'm in charge.* The phrase continued to echo in Monsignor's head long after the meeting was over.

23

"The last time I had crackers for lunch was on August 9, 1990," Guillermo said as he sat down on one of the benches right outside the clinic building.

"How can you remember that?" Isabella asked.

"I'll never forget that day. The night prior, the Prime Minister announced the new government's super-harsh economic program to stabilize hyperinflation."

"Oh, yeah, I remember now. He even finished his speech saying: "God help us."

"Exactly! the next morning gas prices had increased thirty times. In one day, Peru's currency had lost most of its value. That day after school my friend Mario and I put together all the money in our pockets just to afford a package of crackers we shared for lunch."

"A few crackers, that's all you ate the whole day?"

He grabbed a cracker and smiled. "Yeah. Tough times."

Isabella finished her chips and her soda, but before going back to the unit she needed to hear his thoughts. "Well, what do you think?"

"You mean what I think about the two patients that died with marks on their bodies? I actually don't know. I doubt there is something evil behind it. There must be another rational explanation."

Isabella was going to ask what to do next, when she spotted a tall and slender figure with blonde hair and fair skin walking towards them. *Oh no, Andrea! And it looks like she is coming this way! I don't really want to talk to her right now!*

"Hi guys! Time for a snack, right? I needed to get some chips too!"

Isabella had met Andrea when the two of them shared the same cadaver for anatomy class during their second year of medical school. A friendship soon developed. For various reasons they were not as close as they once were.

"How have you been, Isabella?" Andrea said as she opened a bag of potato chips.

"I've been good. Thank you. Very busy. On my medicine ward rotation."

"I left a couple of messages with your Mom, but you never called me back. We should hang out sometime. Maybe you can attend one of our group meetings. Are you free this Friday? I could pick you up."

Isabella did not look at Andrea directly. "I'm sorry I never called you. It's been busy here." Her tone was flat. "I really appreciate you telling me, but I'm kind of focused on this rotation right now." She looked at Guillermo. *Do not leave me, please. I don't really want to talk to her right now.*

"Have you been to mass lately? "Andrea tried again. "We used to go together. These days I usually go with my Dad and Mom to the ten-o'clock service, but we could go to the six-o'clock one, like old times. It's still so much fun with music and lots of young people."

Andrea had a sincere, sweet smile. She wore her hair tied back in a ponytail and was wearing a blue dress under her lab coat.

Isabella realized she was shaking her feet nervously. "It's been a while."

"You went to a Catholic school. You don't want to steer away from your faith for too long."

Remember not to take things personally. She is actually a nice person. "Yes, I did go to a Catholic school. Same as you. And the education was pretty good for the most part."

"So what's wrong?"

"Nothing is wrong. I've just been a little too busy. I'll probably start going to mass again during my next rotation. I'm doing an elective one and I'll have more time off." She knew her answer was not entirely honest but it was time to end the conversation in a nice, polite way. "Maybe we can hang out then. I'll call you, I promise."

Andrea put the unfinished bag of chips inside her blue fanny pack. "Okay then. See you later."

As Andrea was leaving, Isabella turned her head towards Guillermo. "I think I should talk to Casals."

"I'm not sure that is a good idea. What can he do about it?" He said.

"I don't know. Let's go back. I need to finish my notes. "

She got up and was adjusting the fanny pack around her waist when she noticed the morgue guy standing outside one of the office buildings staring at her with a smile.

24

The small side window of Captain Raymundo Vidal's office had been broken for two weeks now, making the room unwelcomely cold. Nothing he could do at this time. The DINCOTE, the police division in charge of fighting terrorist activity, had a very limited budget. The last few weeks had been much busier than usual. The paramilitary death squad known as the Frenchies had increased their level of activity, making the situation even more confusing. To complicate matters, all the evidence was telling him that the chain of command was going all the way up to the head of military intelligence and the President's right hand, general Valentin Montero, "The Doc."

Vidal had just sat down at his desk and was about to start writing his report on the last Shining Path assault, when somebody knocked on the door.

A young police officer interrupted Vidal's thoughts. "Excuse me, captain, do you have a moment?"

"What is it Ramirez?"

"The intelligence group next door is requesting some backup to continue full surveillance in a house in Surco."

"Surco? What's going on in Surco?"

"They didn't say, sir."

"Very interesting," he said, rubbing on his unshaved chin.

The intelligence group never asks for back-up; this has to be important, he thought. Maybe something related to Abimael Guzman or someone of his inner circle. Most people believed that the founder and leader of Shining Path was hiding in some rural area in the Andes. Wasn't it smarter to operate from Lima? Surco is a quiet, middle-class district; nobody would think about looking for him there.

"I've checked the address of the house and it belongs to a young woman." Ramirez hesitated for a moment. "A ballet dancer."

"A dancer?" Could it be possible that Guzman is hiding at a ballerina's house in Surco? Sounds way too crazy to be true. "You can go and offer your help if you want to. But bring me your report on last week's Frenchies activities before you leave."

"Okay, Captain."

"And be sure your radio is working. We're having a lot of issues with the equipment lately."

"Captain, some of the equipment is so old," he said timidly.

"Unfortunately, our budget is very limited. Keep me informed, okay?"

As the young man left, he kept thinking what the chances were that Guzman could be this close. *I better check with the guys next door. They may need the help of an old, crabby policeman.*

25

"Juan Carlos, I'm so happy you made it," said Eduardo La Mota as he welcomed Bishop Silvestri to his beautiful home in the upscale district of San Isidro.

"Thank you for the invitation, my friend." Despite his busy agenda, not for a moment had Bishop Silvestri considered missing this party. He leant over to give a hug to his old friend. Silvestri was tall with wide shoulders, and most people would agree still had the imposing physique from when he was an athlete in high school. However, it was the glacial powerful stare of his green eyes that had become the most compelling tool to dominate any conversation. As he did for most of these reunions outside the church, he wore a black dress shirt with the white clerical collar and black pleated pants.

"I appreciate you coming all the way from Ayacucho to be here. This is an important day for us." La Mota had organized a small family gathering to celebrate that his younger brother had been named the new head of the Ministry of Health.

"I have so many business matters to attend to in Lima that it's not difficult to find an excuse to come here." The priest said as he saluted the other guests with a big smile. He was after all the most charismatic representative of the church and the news media treated him like a celebrity. Silvestri and Eduardo La Mota became friends while attending the same elementary school, and had remained close despite choosing very different careers and living in very different worlds. Silvestri had even made special arrangements so he could be the priest who baptized La Mota's children. "Eduardo, you have a beautiful and successful family. Congratulations!"

"Thank you, Juan Carlos." He looked around proudly. "I think my Dad would have been very pleased."

"He's looking at you with great pride right now, I can tell you that!"

La Mota's Father had been a wealthy entrepreneur. His older son chose to continue in charge of the family business while the younger one, Augusto, became a successful general surgeon.

"Thank you. Now, it's time to open something special to honor this day," he said, while checking the time on his wrist watch. Then he grabbed a bottle of Johnnie Walker Blue Label from his bar cabinet.

"Augusto, come over here!" he yelled. "I was saving this bottle for a special celebration!"

"A Blue Label? I didn't know they made those."

"It has just been released this year. Not easy to find and incredibly expensive," he said as he poured a glass for his younger brother.

Silvestri was more interested in the golden timepiece with black dial and bezel that Eduardo was wearing. "Is that a Tag Heuer?"

Eduardo looked at the priest with surprised eyes and a smile. "I didn't know you were into watches."

"I'm interested in so many things. I noticed your watch. Very unique-looking piece."

"Thank you." La Mota looked at the steel watch with blue and red bezel and yellow dial around Silvestri's wrist. "I see you're wearing a chronograph. But I'm not familiar with the model."

"Yes. This Seiko model is somewhat famous for being worn by an American astronaut on a space flight. It was a present from my Father."

"Salud, brother!" interrupted Augusto, raising his glass. "For the old man, who always thought I was not as smart as my older brother".

"Stop that," said Eduardo, clearly irritated. "Can't we just celebrate your achievements without bringing up the past?"

Augusto sipped on his Scotch and then paused for a second. "Alright then. Let's change topics." His face gradually turned serious. "Maybe this is not the right time, but I wanted to ask you about that guy. The Doc. And maybe it's a good idea to have Father Silvestri here with us, since he has a lot of friends in the military. I'm hoping that as a minister of health I don't need to deal with him at all. But just in case, is there anything I should be aware of?"

Eduardo finished his whisky slowly and played with some of the little ice cubes in his mouth. He didn't look extremely excited to discuss that issue.

"We should probably go to the office," he said, as he got up from his chair. "Let's bring the bottle of whisky."

"I'm sorry. Maybe it's not a good time to talk about it," Augusto said.

"It's alright. We may not have another opportunity. Please come with us, Juan Carlos."

Father Silvestri nodded. He didn't mind at all. He knew that knowledge is power and was always open to acquire more.

Unlike the rest of the house, the office was not overly decorated. A regular-looking desk and shelves with books were overwhelmed by the multitude of diplomas and awards hanging from the walls.

"Valentin Montero is the president's most valuable collaborator. Most people know him as The Doc," Eduardo explained. "His intelligence officers call him The General. I can tell you he's not a doctor. Nor a general. Officially, The Doc is just another behind-the-scenes legal advisor, but in reality, he's the head of military intelligence. Nobody knows much about him. Only what I hear from business people and government friends. Third-party rumors. He's very secretive. Doesn't give any interviews. I do know this: The Doc is dangerous. Avoid him at all costs, and if you have to deal with him, do not trust him."

"I can't agree more with what your brother is saying," said the priest. "I met him once briefly at an embassy reception maybe a year ago. You know that I more than anybody hate all kinds of superstitions, but there is something evil about him."

"By the way, Doc has an expensive watch collection. The one time that I happened to be in the same room with him he was wearing a very nice Cartier," Eduardo said while making himself another drink. "In essence, he's the real person in charge. He has a network of spies working for him at all levels. They are infiltrated everywhere, even in some of the most powerful private companies. In my opinion, he probably has more power than the president himself."

"How did he become close to the president?" Augusto asked

Eduardo grabbed a box of cigars sitting on the coffee table and offered one to his brother. "The Doc defended him in court in some shady real estate business. Nobody knows all the details. He began his career in the Army but was sent to prison for one year after he was found selling secret information to the CIA. Remember in the early seventies, Peru was the only left-wing dictatorship regime in South America. Our president those days, General Velasco, spent large amounts of money buying armaments from the Soviet Union. They say he was getting ready to wage war against Chile. Obviously, this was extremely important to the United States, since that could break the balance in the region. It was a big spying scandal. Some people believe he still has connections to the American government. And maybe that was the reason he got out of jail pretty quickly. Shortly after he started practicing as a lawyer, although there's no clear indication that he ever completed his studies. He had enrolled in law school and somehow obtained a law diploma rather quickly; however, all his records and grades are no longer available at the school archives."

"And that is the man giving advice to the president? Fucking unbelievable! This shit can only happen in Peru!" Augusto said.

Eduardo stared for a few seconds at the picture of his Father on the desk. As he slowly lit the cigar, he said with an ominous voice: "Listen to me, Augusto, don't trust The Doc. The telephone in your soon-to-be office is probably already tapped by him."

Silvestri raised his eyebrows. "The phone line? Are you serious? That's illegal!"

"He can hear everybody's conversations. He's able to discover his enemies' most profound secrets and weaknesses. Don't trust The Doc, little brother!"

26

Isabella looked at the white clock on the kitchen wall. It was almost seven in the evening. It's good to be home early for once, she thought, as her Mom welcomed her with a big hug.

"I made *aji de gallina*, one of your favorites, isn't it? Why don't you go wash your hands and sit at the table and have dinner with me?" Work had been in non-stop mode since the beginning of the medicine rotation, and chances for chit chat between Mother and daughter were becoming more and more infrequent.

"Nothing I'd love more right now, Mom."

But even away from work, in the restful environment of her own house, the image of Mrs. Jimenez' face continued to appear on and off in her thoughts. Against Guillermo's advice she had decided to approach Dr. Casals with her concerns. Although he paid attention to what she had to say, he did not suggest any actions other than to continue to be alert for new cases. It was nice that he listened to her patiently, but still he was not able to hide his skepticism.

"You look a little distracted. How was your day?"

"It was good, Mom."

"You've been pretty busy. Often coming home late. Haven't had much time to talk to you for a while."

"Things are going well, Mom. My attending Dr. Casals is very good. I really like him." She took a bite of the *aji de gallina*. "This is so delicious, Mom. Where is Dad?" She had not seen her Father in days.

"You know, he has been very busy at work," Mrs. Castle said. Isabella thought she was just making excuses for him. How could he be so busy at work? Rumors say he was not being a loyal husband. And probably her Mom knew it, but didn't say anything. *Wasn't this how all Peruvian men behave at the end anyway?*

"Have you heard from Diego?" Isabella not only wanted to change the topic but she missed her brother enormously.

"The postcard I showed you a week ago is the last time I heard from him. But no worries, your brother is fine. He knows how to take care of himself. I know he's fine. Maybe he found a girlfriend."

"Or a boyfriend." Isabella couldn't stop herself. She hated to contradict her Mother, especially at a time like this, when she looked alone and unhappy, but she was also tired of ignoring reality.

"Isabella, stop it! Don't talk like that!"

"Why does everybody keep avoiding the subject? Diego is gay, Mom, you have to accept it and love him for what he is and hope he finds happiness."

"We don't know that, we don't know that he isn't straight. I know he likes girls. He had girlfriends before."

"He had one girlfriend. When he was in kindergarten, I think. That wasn't a real girlfriend." But Isabella didn't have the energy to continue arguing. "But that's okay, Mom. We still love him. I'm not so sure about Dad, but you and I love him and miss him, and that's what is important."

"What do you mean?" Mrs. Castle frowned in disapproval. "Of course your Dad loves your brother. If you're having those ideas, I think you should talk to him."

Isabella did not say anything else. She felt bad for her. She knew her Mom adored Diego and it was very hard for her to let him go to find his future somewhere else. And she was probably afraid one day her daughter was going to leave her, too. She took another bite of the *aji de gallina.*

"It's good to see you eating well."

"Oh, I was starving!"

"You haven't been to therapy or taking any meds for more than six months. How are you feeling? Are you holding okay? You know we can always make an appointment for therapy, like for a mainte-nance follow-up."

Isabella has not thought about her depression for a while. As she stared at the clock on the wall one more time, the memory of some of her old unresolved feelings came back to her.

"I'm okay, Mom."

She can see herself again. It feels like it was yesterday. She is sitting at her therapist's office. Hoping that the appointment never ends. She looks at the clock on the wall. It has already been an hour and the session will be over soon.

"Today will be our last meeting," says the woman with a firm but friendly voice.

"I know."

"You've been coming to see me once a month for the last two years. How does it feel to be released to be on your own?"

"It feels good."

"Being discharged means no more regular follow-ups, but we can always see you if you need to. You know that, right?"

"Yes."

"How long have you been off your antidepressants now?"

"Three months."

"And are you feeling okay?"

"I feel okay."

"I understand you are going to start your internship soon."

"It's actually the year before the internship. They call it sub- internship."

"But still very demanding physically and mentally, correct?"

"Yes."

"Understand, you are gonna be at risk of a relapse, that's a reality. Overwhelming stress will always put you at risk. I wanted you to know that you can always call and make an appointment and I'll see you as soon as I can. You understand?"

"I do."

"Are you excited? I know you have been waiting for this."

"Yes, I'm excited. Medicine is very competitive and I don't think I've performed at my best yet. I really want to show everybody how good of a doctor I am."

"You look sad. Don't be sad. I'm always here for you, okay?"

"Okay. I think I'm just afraid," she says, with tears in her eyes.

"I know and that's okay. It's okay to be afraid. You know that, right?"

"I do."

"Before you leave, Isabella. Would you give me a hug?"

"Isabella!"

It feels like it was yesterday.

"Isabella! Her Mother's voice jarred her back to the present. "What's wrong? Are you crying?"

"I'm okay, Mom," she replied with tears in her eyes.

27

Archbishop Villena-Alarcon could not hide his joy as he stepped out of the vehicle bringing him to Colegio de la Inmaculada Concepción, the place that for many years saw him grow as an educator, theological scholar and spiritual leader. It felt like being back home.

The Archbishop had also been one of the original founders of the new school campus. Two decades ago, his energetic networking skills had secured the final donations that made it possible to move from a very modest building in downtown Lima to a state-of-the-art facility in the young upscale district of La Molina.

Father Esteban Alcazar, the school headmaster, was waiting for him outside the main office building. He was a small man with dark hair and gray beard that spoke calmly using elegant words. Villena-Alarcon had called multiple times before being able to schedule an appointment with him. Alcazar had proposed a different location for the encounter, but the old priest had insisted on coming to the school.

"Good morning, Esteban."

"Good morning, Monsignor. We're very honored with your visit."

"Please Esteban, stop with the formalities. Why don't you show me how the construction for the new library is going? It's been a couple of years now since the last time I visited the school. We can talk as we walk .We should take advantage before starts raining again." Villena -Alarcon said while looking at the dark clouds above them.

"I'm inclined to think that you want to talk about Silvestri and Opus Dei." The Archbishop knew it was Father Alcazar's approach to go straight to the point.

"You're a smart man, Esteban." The old priest grinned, pleased with his openness. "That's why I'm here. I need your advice. I understand that due to some incidents in the past, some people have the impression that Opus Dei and our Order of Jesus do not get along, and I don't want to reinforce that view."

"Some people may think that we are jealous of the special treatment their group is getting from Pope John Paul II," said Esteban in an ironic tone.

"I know, I know. But Opus Dei also has a history of being extremely friendly with right wing and fascist dictatorships. Several members of Opus Dei worked in high government positions in Francisco Franco's Spain. So the similarities are undeniable, our president with the support of the military dissolves congress and the judiciary branch likely unconstitutionally, becoming a de facto dictator. Opus Dei not only doesn't show any signs of uneasiness but instead conveys their support and now Augusto La Mota, an Opus Dei supernumerary , assumes the position of new Ministry of Health. Doesn't it look to you like history is repeating again?"

"Indeed, Monsignor. But you must act with extreme caution. Opus Dei has powerful friends in Rome."

The Archbishop stopped for a second, took a deep breath and looked around the beautiful gardens and the modern buildings. "I loved it here, you know. Sometimes I wish I stayed working for the school; my life would be much more simple."

28

The ride to the hospital could have been less of a reminder of a medical student's dreary routine if Mario had chosen some different kind of music. Guillermo kept thinking that having Queen's "Who Wants to Live Forever" playing in the background during an overcast, rainy day would not be his preferred selection to elevate his mood. His dear friend only had two cassettes in the glovebox of his Mazda 323, Def Leppard's "Pyromania" and Queen's "Greatest Hits," which he played over and over.

"It's a great song. It's on the Highlander's soundtrack." Mario said.

"I know. You told me before. I haven't seen the movie yet. I guess for me it's just a sad song." He tried to be positive; this was still far better than having to take the bus and waste forty minutes of his life in a crowded tuna can.

The Pathology session was held once a month in one of the large auditorium halls. A recent case from the hospital was presented. The history, abnormal lab results, imaging and possible diagnostic possibilities were discussed briefly and then a Pathology professor went over the microscopic tissue samples either from a biopsy site or, if the unfortunate patient didn't make it alive, from an autopsy specimen. The goal was to be able to visualize how the clinical manifestations correlated with the changes at the smaller tissue levels.

"The freaking explosion blasted my windows. It was so loud, my friend. Really scary shit." Hector Yamamoto, one of the two students of Japanese background, explained as they walked in and looked for some empty seats. The most recent terrorist incident had brought down a power tower and left a quarter of the city with no electricity.

"Another week and another explosion and another power outage. I'm tired of having to read by candlelight," Mario said.

"In one way or another, this feeling of insecurity is affecting every single person, my friend." Guillermo knew from personal experience. He looked around and saw the same familiar faces he'd known from day one of medical school. They represented a very diverse population: from upper-class kids educated in expensive private and Catholic schools to students that attended poor public schools, many of them members of immigrant families from the Peruvian Andes, the area that the people from the more affluent coastal cities called, sometimes in a derogatory way, *la sierra*.

Being from an economically weakened and shrinking middle-class family from Lima, Guillermo felt a little bit of an outsider and his circle of friends had remained relatively small.

"You know, Alfonso's Dad received a letter from Shining Path asking his company for five-thousand dollars a month to contribute to their cause, otherwise something bad will happen to him or his family; can you believe it?" Mario asked.

"That's terrible! I'm so sorry for him! What is he doing? Is he paying? Five-thousand dollars a month is a lot of money!"

"I don't know, but they have hired a private security company. Alfonso was driven to work by a bodyguard this morning."

"Something that also makes me sad is how nobody in the rest of the world is aware of what's happening here. Johnny Fishman just came from the United States; his Dad took the family to Disneyworld in Orlando and he was watching this cable news channel called CNN and there were absolutely no stories about Peru. It looks like for most of the world, we are just another irrelevant, developing country."

"The United States is dealing with its own issues, you know? A lot of social unrest. Have you heard about the LA riots?"

"No, no really."

"I wonder if there is gonna be any country left by the time we are ready to go into medical practice."

"You better start thinking about immigrating, my friend: Spain and the United States are probably the best options." Mario spoke sincerely. He was already looking into taking the American Board exams. "This country is going to hell, my friend. I'm not staying here. And I hope I can eventually get my family out, too."

Guillermo knew that some of his classmates were considering leaving the country and were getting ready to start the long process. He didn't know what to do. Even if he wanted, was he going to be able to afford it? In order to prepare he had to study from multiple costly books, one for each preclinical and clinical course, and then find a way to finance the two expensive exams plus the travel expenses, since the testing sites were available in the United States only. And his Father, always having difficulty making ends meet, was unlikely to be able to help him.

"But that's so sad. It doesn't have to be that way. Despite all the bad things, I really love it here," Guillermo explained.

"What is it that you love so much?"

"Well, I love the food and…" he paused for a second, thinking. "I guess I love going to the beach in the summer…and my family is here."

Mario laughed. "That didn't sound entirely convincing to me."

"I guess not," he shrugged.

"You know what?" Mario's voice was uplifting now. "Fuck Shining Path. Let's go to Barranco on Friday, let's go have a beer, I'll pick you up!"

"What happened to Annie? Are you guys still dating?"

"Annie is a no-go." Mario laughed. "Seriously. Too needy."

"Alright, then, but I'm choosing the music this time."

29

Archbishop Villena-Alarcon did not get the advice that he'd hoped for. As the two Jesuit priests walked down the stairs of the modern new library, he knew it was time to finish his visit and go back to the Archdiocese.

"Thank you for having me, Esteban. As always, your advice has been sincere and rational, but also a little more conservative than I expected."

"It's because I believe the conservative approach is the best approach right now."

"I will speak to some of the other bishops and bring up my concerns in a way that does not sound like I'm becoming a paranoid conspiracy theorist. In any way, it was very nice to be back at the school. So many great memories. Thank you again."

As they walked outside the main building, the black Lincoln Town Car was already waiting for him.

"My pleasure, Monsignor. Give me a call if you need anything. Better get on your way, traffic to downtown Lima is going to get pretty busy soon." There was some sadness in Esteban's voice.

"Good afternoon, Father." The chauffeur said while gently holding the door open. As the Archbishop got in the car, he saw a younger figure approaching Father Esteban.

"Was that the Archbishop that just left? What is he doing here? I don't think it's a good thing for him to come here…" the young man said.

The car drove away and Monsignor Villena-Alarcon was not able to hear the entire conversation, but from the distance he could see Father Esteban's face color had quickly turned into a choleric red.

He lowered his head with resignation. It was clear he was not welcomed there anymore.

30

The door nameplate said *Dr. Alejandro Cazorla, Dean* in golden letters.

Jorge Casals didn't feel exactly at home. The place was a bit more elegant than he remembered. The medical school administration offices looked much nicer than...when was the last time he was here... five years ago? New carpets, expensive dark wood bookshelves, they even got a pretty secretary with a cute smile answering the phone. But after twenty-five minutes of waiting, he was becoming a little impatient when the door finally opened.

"Sorry for making you wait, Jorge. Please come on in."

"Thank you for seeing me, Alejandro."

"No problem at all. Please have a seat."

Cazorla's office was also tastefully decorated. A brass lamp with the university logo stood on the hand carved mahogany desk.

"How can I help you?" For a second, he felt Cazorla looked at his clothes with disapproval.

Although the same age, he appeared to be a few years younger than Casals. With his bushy light-brown hair, jovial eyes, elegant fashion sense and with the tendency to grandiloquent speeches, Alejandro Cazorla was the perfect face for the school of medicine.

"There has been another case, Alejandro. This time it wasn't what I'd called a patient with a terminal condition like the previous ones, but instead an older woman with a treatable illness."

Cazorla's welcoming smile was all but gone.

"Something was new, though," Casals added. "In all the other cases the black cross was found in the chest or in the back. This time it was clearly visible on the patient's cheek."

"On the face? Who would do that?"

"I'm afraid our subject is feeling less restrictive about his choices, and not only that, leaving his mark clearly noticeable on the patient, I'm worried it could mean that he's looking for some attention. I don't think we should wait any longer. I think this is the time when you need to get the police involved."

Cazorla looked down and shook his head in disagreement. "Please give me a little more time to figure this thing out. I have my security people investigating. Nobody else knows about it yet. I've been working closely with La Mota, the hospital director, who is an old friend of mine. He's also asking me to keep the police out of this for the moment. He doesn't want some sensationalistic newspaper printing this crap right around the time he swears in as the new Minister of Health."

"One of our students just realized that something isn't right."

"What do you mean?"

"There's a student that noticed the cross on the last victim. She had also seen a similar one last year in a cachectic terminal man."

"Who is this student we are talking about?"

"Her name is Isabella Castle. She's part of my team."

"I know who she is. History of severe depression. A few years ago, she was admitted to the psych ward. She almost had to quit medicine."

"She's a very intelligent girl and I wouldn't be surprised if she soon discovers there is a serial murderer killing patients in our hospital."

"We need to stay calm. Listen, this is what we know so far. There have been five cases, all of them were elderly and debilitated. No families have come forward to complain, which is good and gives us time. I'm thinking this is a case of what they call an 'angel of mercy.' Similar cases in other countries have found that the perpetrator is usually a caregiver or a nurse that kills as a way to minimize the patient's agony."

"That doesn't match our most recent case."

"It could be a small variation. Most cases I believe have happened at night, so we are looking mostly at the night-shift nursing staff."

"Why only nurses? Would it be possible for a physician or a resident to be responsible?"

"My God! You are not serious, right? We are doctors. We're a different species. We dedicate our lives to save people's lives, not the other way around! Please help me out here. Tell this Castle girl that it was probably just a weird coincidence, come up with something, you'll figure it out. Again, the hospital security team is going to continue the investigation. If the police were to intervene right now, then it is just a matter of days before the media learns of this and our hospital reputation goes down the drain."

Casals hesitated for a moment. This was his old friend, after all, and he was asking for a favor. "Okay, let's do as you say then."

"One more thing. My old friend Carlos Meneses is now the head of Chelsea Laboratories in Peru. He asked me if I had a recommendation for a medical director and I mentioned your name. What do you think? Chelsea is ready to launch Vancomycin in Peru. It's just a matter of time before MRSA becomes a problem here like it is becoming everywhere in the developed world, and Vancomycin is the only available antibiotic that works. I can see you giving a lot of lectures and traveling a lot. It probably pays five times more than what you are earning right now between the hospital and the office."

The offer took Casals by surprise.

"Thank you. That sounds very interesting, but I really love the hospital and teaching."

"We can figure something out. I could talk to La Mota, you could stay as a member of the staff and round with your team maybe once a week as a guest faculty. I'm sure we can arrange something that will keep everybody happy. What do you say? I'll tell Meneses to schedule an interview."

"Appreciate the offer, Alejandro." He stood up. It was time for this meeting to be over. "Thank you very much for considering me. I have to go back to the hospital now."

"Very well, let me accompany you."

For Casals, it was hard to believe how these two men, once young and idealistic, have grown apart so much.

"You should think about my offer, Jorge. It could be a very good deal for you."

Casals looked at Cazorla's expensive dark gray business suit as the Dean held the office's door open for him. He noticed the buttoned-down coat.

"Do something for me, okay?" Casals said. "When wearing a two-button jacket, always leave the lower one unbuttoned. It's one of those non-written sartorial rules. It actually goes all the way back to King Edward VII."

31

Standing outside the hospital lab, waiting for stat results on a patient, Isabella could see Mrs. Jimenez' sweet smile and gentle touch popping into her head every five minutes. Casals told her not to worry about it. That it was probably some weird coincidence. The fact that she was second-guessing herself was making her irritable. On top of everything she needed to deal with the system's inefficiency. *This fucking lab is so slow. Come back in one hour, they said! How am I going to replace electrolytes in the alcohol withdrawal patient before he develops an irregular heartbeat?*

She made eye contact with a familiar face passing by wearing an all-white dress shirt and pants underneath the lab coat. The unofficial uniform of the OB/GYN residents.

"Hi there," said Martin Benitez.

"I didn't know you got into an OB/GYN residency. How are things going?"

"Very well, actually."

Although math and organic chemistry had been really painful classes, nothing compared to the miserable days that Isabella endured during the OB/GYN rotation. She thought her team members were a bunch of *chauvinistic assholes*. Not good for being the only woman around. The nonstop harassment from attendings and residents during the never-ending obstetric calls. If something was clear by the end of the rotation, it was that the OB/GYN was not the specialty for her.

"In a few months, I've already done over ten C-sections" he said.

Like some other surgical specialties, the quality of training was measured in part by the number of procedures the residents were able to do.

"Hey, do you remember that older man that had a cardiac arrest on the medical ward about a year ago? I was going to one of my classes when that happened and I stayed to help with chest compressions. You were the intern."

"Yeah, I know what patient you're talking about. What about it?"

"Do you remember this man had a small black cross painted on his chest?"

"No, sorry." Benitez shook his head. "I don't remember that."

"It's okay. Not a big deal." She looked down, disappointed.

"I've got to go now. They asked me to help with a vaginal hyster-ectomy. I'll see you around. Stop by the unit to say hi some time."

"Absolutely!" She smiled, knowing she was going to stay as far away as possible from the OB/GYN building.

"What's that, one of your OB/GYN buddies?" said Guillermo as he walked towards her.

"No, just an old intern that chose the dark path of the vagina."

"You know, you can be very funny sometimes," he said laughing.

"Well, I'm not in a good mood. I've been waiting for these stat labs forever."

"Looks like they are very behind today. The hospital workers union are debating going on strike. Let's hope it doesn't happen."

"That'll be bad news. You wanna hang out with me here while I'm waiting?"

"Sure."

"Thank you."

"Looks like you don't really like OB/GYN."

'Some of what they do can be very interesting. I just didn't have a good experience during my rotation. Do you know what specialty you wanna practice in the future?"

"No. I don't know yet. Nothing surgical for sure," he laughed. "Nothing against surgeons. Being in the OR is just not my thing. Actually, my good friend Mario wants to be a surgeon. What about you?"

"Some internal medicine subspecialty most likely."

"Hey, I was listening when you were talking to Andrea the other day about not going to church any more. Is it because you're just too busy and tired or you actually don't feel like being religious anymore?"

She'd been asked the same question a few times now. Any hints of possibly being a non-believer were definitely unusual these days in the overwhelmingly Catholic Peruvian society.

"Last time I went to mass, the priest was talking about how women had to make an effort to stay pretty and fit, wear makeup and everything possible for your husband to stay attracted to you so he doesn't cheat."

"Well..." he started saying.

"So, it's women's fault that men cheat. Great advice, Father, thank you. I'll see you next Sunday."

"It sounds like he meant well; all he wanted is for couples to stay together and…"

"Never mind," she interrupted. "Why were you asking?"

"I was wondering if you consider yourself an agnostic. Mario is a passionate agnostic. Pretty much the only one I know. He's been rather unsuccessful in his efforts to convert me to his cause," he said smiling. "I always wonder if there are actually more people like him and they just keep it to themselves. Are you an agnostic too?"

"I don't know," she shrugged. "There are many things about organized religion that I don't agree with." She paused for a few seconds. "Maybe I'd like to believe there is a God."

"It's interesting that before going to med school I had not really met anyone that didn't consider themselves Catholic."

"That happens when you grow up in a Catholic family and attend a Catholic school."

"Inside a Catholic bubble?" He laughed. "I guess that's true. You think the whole world is the same way. I hope I'm not asking uncomfortable questions, but what is it that makes it so hard to believe?" He appeared sincerely interested to hear more about it.

"No, it's okay." In a way she welcomed the opportunity of talking about this. Not too many people were willing to listen without judging.

"I just think I'm going through a period in my life where I have a lot of questions and doubts. I grew up in a very Catholic family. My grandmother was extremely devout of Señor *de los Milagros*. I used to go to Sunday mass with my family every week. I went to a Catholic school."

"*Señor de los Milagros!* It's funny you mentioned him. My grandma wears the purple dress every day during the month of October. Did something happen to change your opinion about religion?"

"A few things, I guess. I have a brother. Have I told you about him?"

"No, I don't think so."

"Well, it's kind of a long story. It's better if I tell you some other day."

Only after a few interminable seconds of awkward silence, he said, "I could talk to Carlos Salazar, he's one of the leaders of the student's Catholic group, maybe he can help or maybe he can invite you to one of their meetings."

Isabella was used to this reaction. There is something wrong with you for having doubts, you should talk to this person who is really an expert in this matter. He may help you to become normal again.

"That's okay. My friend Andrea has joined that group, too. But to be honest, this Carlos friend of yours, there's something about him that I don't like."

"I hear you. He can be a bit of a jerk sometimes, but I can tell you that he and his group do some good social work. A few weekends ago, for example, they volunteered to help with a vaccination campaign for poor kids in Villa El Salvador."

A lab tech handed her a two-page chemistry results.

"Hey, lab results are back!"

32

Isabella finished her work that day much later than usual. Her Mother had kindly left some *estofado* on the table ready for her to warm up, but she was not feeling really hungry. She did not see her Dad's car, so she assumed he was working late again. Her parents' relationship had continued to deteriorate since around the time Diego had left. *Diego. What are you doing right now, brother?* She walked down the hallway and carefully opened the door of her brother's bedroom. Everything looked just exactly the way it did before he left. A shelf with a few of his favorite books: García Marquez' *Crónica de una muerte anunciada*, Vargas Llosa's *La Ciudad y los Perros*, Jorge Luis Borges' *Ficciones*. Some old toys, the Corgi Toys Batmobile. Even Cindy Crawford's poster was still there. Like she always did, she looked through his collection of vinyl records. They pretty much shared the same music taste: Blondie, The Clash, Soda Stereo, The Police, U2. She grabbed Gary Numan's album *The Pleasure Prince*. The picture of Numan on the cover reminded her of Diego. She could almost picture her brother's face wearing eyeliner. Like before, she played a song named "*M.E.*" Diego used to listen all the time. She closed her eyes. It was like she could feel his presence. *I wish you were here, Diego... I'm feeling so alone sometimes.*

She wondered when was the last time she felt like everything was fine. Midway through high school maybe? Things were so easy before that. And then the challenges started to happen in rapid succession and at some point, depression started taking over. Medical school was already very hard even before the realization that medicine is a field dominated by men that become very nervous next to talented, outspoken women. Breaking up with her long-term boyfriend. Therapy and antidepressants. And after that, the news that Diego was not gonna be in the bedroom next door no more. And now it's not even clear if Mom and Dad were still in love with each other.

I wish you were here, Diego.

33

Bishop Juan Carlos Silvestri smiled for the camera flashes, next to the mayor of the city of Ayacucho and the new Ministry of Health doctor Augusto La Mota as they uncovered the commemorative plate for the inauguration of the brand-new Children's Hospital. The government had to be sure that appropriate news coverage was given to the event, and recruiting the charismatic clergyman was an effective way to bring more attention to it. The building, which still smelt like fresh paint, was one of the promises of the president as a candidate, and he needed to score a few points with public opinion.

"Very nice hospital, Augusto."

"Thank you, Father."

"I have a few concerns, though. I've seen some areas that do not appear completely finished. Some others with missing equipment. Are you sure this place is ready to go?

"Absolutely, Father. A lot of the equipment will be added gradually," he said without stopping smiling for the photographers.

"I was also told that the hospital may not have the number of nurses and doctors needed to run efficiently."

"I've been to multiple meetings with the hospital directors and they are working to solve that as we speak. We'd like to be able to offer every single pediatric specialty."

"The whole thing feels a little rushed, but I hope everything works out well."

"Thank you, Father."

"When are you going back to Lima?"

"This afternoon."

"Perhaps you can join us for lunch at the Diocese; we have an excellent cook."

"That would be great, but unfortunately I have to attend a meeting with the hospital board."

"Unfortunate, indeed," the Bishop said. "You're very brave to come to Ayacucho. Somewhere out there, Shining Path militants are planning their next attack."

"It's crazy to think that Abimael Guzman could just be a few miles away from here."

"I actually believe he's not in Ayacucho anymore. I have a theory that he's in Lima now."

La Mota raised an eyebrow. "Why do you think that?"

"I've spent a lot of time studying Guzman and the Shining Path. In order to better fight your enemy, you should learn as much about them as you can. Or at least that's what Sun Tzu says. Right?"

"Who? I'm not really sure."

"Guzman is a smart person. Let's not forget when he came here in the sixties, he was actually a university philosophy professor. As with many other intellectuals in Latin America, his initially noble ideals for a more equitable society eventually led him to embrace communism."

"That's true, I have many well-educated friends, some of them university professors, that supported socialism and the Cuban revolution."

"They were trendy ideologies. Later, however, as Guzman became more politically active, he adopted some of the Mao Tse Tung theories, in which war was necessary to achieve a real transformation of society."

"Those transformative processes almost always involved thousands of people dying."

"You are absolutely right, Augusto. About that time Guzman went underground. Nobody knew where he operated from. The fact that not much was known about the man only helped him to become more of a myth. But most of their activity is now focused in Lima and the surrounding towns. If he, as I think, likes to keep a tight control on Shining Path's activities, it makes more sense to stay close to the action."

"I see. Ayacucho is still dangerous, though. Are you afraid of living here?"

"I'm not afraid of the Shining Path. Guzman would never try to kill a church authority. At least not initially. It would be immensely unpopular among the people and he's too smart to do that. However, if the communists were to obtain power, their goal would be to eventually eliminate religion from society. So, the Catholic Church is in a way under attack too."

"We're all under attack, Father. I'm happy that you're very open about your strong support for the government."

"Thank you, Augusto. And to answer your question earlier—*The Art of War*, by Sun Tzu. One of the main principles is you must learn as much as you can about your enemy. You should read it."

"Most definitely, Father."

"Anyway, you have a good flight back to Lima. Say hi to your brother. I have the feeling we are going to meet again very soon."

34

"Sixty-four-year-old male patient presents with four weeks of progressive shortness of breath, productive cough and weight loss of about twenty kilograms." Guillermo presented the case, standing in front of the attending physician and his medical team peers. "For the last few days the patient also reports coughing up blood as much as a tablespoon every two hours."

"Let's pause right there, Guillermo." Casals said. "As you're listening to the history of present illness, your brain is already processing the information. You have to ask yourselves what conditions could explain shortness of breath, cough and weight loss."

The Socratic method, in which the senior doctor asks a series of guided questions to the students in order to stimulate critical thinking, was the predominant way of teaching on the medical wards. This approach, although effective, can be intense and intimidating for the learner. For Guillermo, who was introverted and quiet at baseline, it had been a work in progress that he had gradually been able to manage.

"What would be the first thing that comes to your mind in terms of diagnosis Hugo?"

"Tuberculosis."

"That is correct. Unfortunately tuberculosis is so prevalent in our country. If you have a patient that presents with a cough with bloody sputum and weight loss, tuberculosis is going to be the diagnosis until proven otherwise. Any history of contacts, Guillermo?"

"No sir. Past medical and social history are pretty much unremarkable. He works as a manager of a supermarket and he's never been a smoker."

"Very good, you are already thinking about the differential diagnosis in your head, right? Shortness of breath, coughing up blood and weight loss, symptoms for about four weeks. "What is the next thing we have to keep in mind, Isabella, especially if there was a history of heavy smoking?"

"Lung cancer?"

"Exactly."

"Let's look at the chest X-ray now. We're gonna let our student Raul describe the findings," he said as Hugo placed the film on the light box.

Raul's face turned red quickly. The young man had just started his rotation with the team, and being on the spot for the first time was clearly overwhelming.

"Let's see," he said, taking a deep breath to regain composure. "It's a postero- anterior view. The chest is slightly rotated to the right; that's why the clavicles are not completely even. Soft tissues and bone structures with no major abnormalities. The heart and the mediastinal silhouette are normal size. No cardiomegaly. No pleural effusions.

There are bilateral perihilar lung infiltrates not very well defined, I'm going to say mostly alveolar. I don't see any masses or cavitary lesions."

"That was a great read, Raul. What specialty did you say you wanted to go to in the future?" Casals asked.

"Radiology, sir."

Everybody but Raul laughed. The young student looked confused.

"That makes our differential diagnosis a little more complicated. Although tuberculosis can present with any kind of pulmonary abnormalities on chest X-ray, we are not seeing the characteristic upper-lobe lung infiltrates with or without cavitation. We also don't see any masses that would make lung cancer less likely. With one exception. Anybody?"

Nobody attempted to answer.

"There is a type of lung cancer called bronchoalveolar cell carcinoma that can present with alveolar infiltrates and look just like pneumonia."

The team members looked at each other, disappointed.

"Let's see if we can get some help from the lab results. Anything significant?" Casals asked again.

"White blood count slightly low, 4,000. Hemoglobin slightly low, 11.5. Creatinine slightly high, 1.6. The urinalysis showed 3+ red blood cells, 3+ protein, no bacteria. Blood and urine cultures are negative."

"Hmm, interesting." Casals rubbed his chin. "The renal function is not normal and the urine has blood and protein. I guess the next question is: are those renal abnormalities related to the pulmonary picture at all, or are they two different, not related things?"

"Maybe they are two different things," Hugo said. "The renal failure might be acute if our guy was a little dehydrated. And maybe he has some blood in the urine from an enlarged prostate."

"Yes, those are possible explanations, but the presence of 3+ protein suggests kidney involvement at the glomerular level."

Nobody said anything. They knew Casals was getting ready to say something brilliant.

"Remember this," he said. "When you approach a difficult-to-diagnose case with multiple manifestations, always try to apply Occam's razor."

They looked at each other confused. What did he just say?

"Generally speaking, Occam's razor says that the most likely explanation is usually the most simple one. The way it applies to our field is trying to explain that all the signs and symptoms are being caused by one single illness rather than multiple ones."

Never heard of it.

"Going back to our case, what condition could explain pulmonary involvement causing hemoptysis and kidney involvement causing increased blood and protein in the urine?"

Everybody remained silent. And then it just came to his mind. "A vasculitis," said Guillermo victoriously.

"Exactly. Vasculitis refers to conditions that can affect and cause inflammation in multiple organs."

"Can you guys name any vasculitis that causes pulmonary and renal involvement?"

"Wegener?" asked Hugo.

"Very good. These are uncommon conditions, but mostly remember Wegener granulomatosis and Goodpasture syndrome.

Ideally you want a biopsy to make the diagnosis. But let's start ordering serologic studies first. Let's also consult pulmonary. I tried not to consult too many specialties, since I want you guys to come out with your own differential diagnosis and plan but in this case, we will probably need a bronchoscopy."

Hugo had finally made a fortunate intervention and could not hide a triumphant smile.

Stop smiling, jerk. I said vasculitis first.

"Okay guys, let's take a break for lunch. Page me if you have any questions," Casals said.

"Those were some of the best teaching rounds ever." Guillermo could not hide his admiration for the attending.

"I agree completely," Isabella said.

"I guess I'm gonna have to read about Occam's razor."

"Hey Guillermo, I wanted to ask you something," Isabella said as they both walked outside the unit. "Have you ever seen the guy that works in the morgue?"

"Are you talking about Igor?"

"Igor? Is that his name? Seriously?"

"No, I don't actually know his real name, but everybody calls him Igor. I picture him like a dungeon guard. What's up with him?"

"He acted kind of weird when I went to see Mrs. Jimenez' body, and I caught him staring at me the other day. I had the impression he was following me."

"Well, I guess he could just find you attractive."

She blushed and looked down. "Whatever. He freaks me out!"

He realized that the compliment had made her feel uncomfortable and tried to quickly change direction.

"You think he's somehow related to these killings?"

"That's what I'm wondering. Can you maybe ask other people if he is known for any unusual habits?"

"His looks are unusual for sure," he said casually.

Isabella didn't reply. She just looked at him with cold eyes. She was obviously taking this matter very seriously.

"Of course, I will."

35

Captain Raymundo Vidal was tired of dealing with the frequent power failures at the DINCOTE's old building. Not enough natural light reached his corner office, and if the electricity was not back soon he was going to have to bring unfinished work home with him. Something he really hated.

"Sorry to interrupt, Captain." The young officer opened the door shyly.

"It's fine. Come on in, Ramirez."

"The intelligence team doesn't have enough field agents so I've been helping out like we spoke. I've been doing surveillance on the ballet dancer's house."

"The house in Surco, yes, I remember. What's happening?"

"Nothing really suspicious. She lives with her fiancé and teaches dance classes to little girls on the first floor."

"Nothing out of the ordinary?"

"The house appears to produce more garbage than you would expect for two people. So, they've been told to examine the trash for clues."

"Examine the trash! Really?"

"Yes, look for any documents or receipts, but especially look for medications or prescriptions."

"Interesting. Such an unusual method." Vidal's eyes narrowed. Maybe it was time to go talk to them.

36

"I don't even know why I keep watching the news anymore. One of these days they're gonna give me a heart attack!" said Archbishop Villena-Alarcon as he got up from his cozy chair to turn the TV off.

"What's wrong, Father?" asked the young man.

"Same old, Armando. The frequent appearances of the unruly Bishop of Ayacucho on national television are making me upset."

"Are you talking about Father Silvestri?"

"Of course, Armando! Same freaking Silvestri! I'm getting tired of him."

The priest washed his hands. He looked at the mirror in front of him. The puffy bags under his eyes were getting more noticeable every day.

"You know what he said this time? He compared Abimael Guzman, the leader of Shining Path, to Pol Pot." He sat back on his chair shaking his head in discontent.

Armando gave him a perplexed look.

"Do you know who Pol Pot is?"

"No Father, I'm sorry, I don't"

"How old are you anyway?" the priest asked with a frown. "Sorry, I can't remember."

"Sixteen, Father."

"Well, I think schools should spend more time talking about contemporary world history. Anyway, Pol Pot was the head of a communist party in Cambodia called Khmer Rouge that was in control of the country in the seventies. The Khmer Rouge government was brutal, leading to the genocide of almost two million people. I'm sure Guzman's going to be very happy with the comparison. He probably loves to get this much attention from the press. At the same time this can only cause more anxiety and fear on the part of the Peruvian people, who are already emotionally overwhelmed."

"What are you going to do, Father?"

"You know, Armando, I've been advised not to do anything, but I don't think I can continue doing nothing for much longer."

"Monsignor?"

"Tell me, Armando."

"Excuse me, Monsignor but your dinner's gonna get cold," he said, while pointing at the food tray on the table.

37

Most people would agree that the colorful gardens of Santa Maria Hospital look beautiful during the day, but as the sun goes down, the tall bushes block all the light on the narrow walkways that connect the medical pavilions with the surrounding buildings.

The moon is hiding tonight. Nobody can see anything with this darkness. A perfect night.

A tall shadow wearing a white lab coat opened the door of Pavilion 5, the surgical ward. He had timed himself, waiting for the two floor nurses to get busy attending a new patient that was just brought after undergoing emergency surgery. As always, he methodically went through the checklist on his mind to be sure everything was in order. The Stranger stopped in front of bed 14. A middle-aged woman appeared to be sleeping, but her face did not show signs of being comfortable. Despite multiple abdominal surgeries, the doctors have not been able to eradicate the ongoing infection. She has not been able to eat for weeks and she had to be fed with intravenous nutrition. Constant pain was difficult to treat and the attending had no problems in using a limited amount of morphine otherwise rarely used due to tight hospital regulations.

The Stranger put on a pair of surgical gloves and grabbed two syringes from his fanny pack. *The first dose will make you sleep, my dear. The second one will stop your breathing. You will feel nothing, I promise.* Then he put the headphones on and pressed play on his Walkman. He closed his eyes as he pushed the drugs in and took a long deep breath.

"I am the eggman, They are the eggman, I am the walrus."

He watched calmly as the woman's breathing slowed down gradually and finally stopped. Then he proceeded to leave his personal mark on the patient's upper chest, next to the central IV line providing parenteral nutrition.

He looked around to be sure nobody was watching and left the building into the blackness of the night.

A perfect night indeed.

38

"Have a good night Dr. Casals!"

"Have a good night Mrs. Consuelo. I'll be leaving soon, too," he told the receptionist.

Casals had just finished seeing the last patient of the day and needed a few minutes to complete his notes. He could not stop feeling uneasy, however.

He kept thinking about his meeting with Cazorla. In a way his old colleague was right. Between the hospital and his office practice, he was barely able to afford to pay the rent and living expenses for his family. His wife was a stay-at-home Mom and their two daughters were not old enough to go to school yet. Is working for a drug company such a bad thing? *Would I be selling my soul to the devil? Am I being too naive for trying to keep the practice of medicine as pure as possible?* He knew that as his daughters grew up, a higher-income job would be needed in the future.

That wasn't the only thing on his mind, though. When Isabella came to talk to him earlier that day, he had said not to worry about things, when in fact he knew that some patients were dying at the hospital in suspicious ways and only his loyalty to Cazorla and the school was making him keep his mouth shut. He had agreed to wait for a reasonable period, but if more deaths occur he may have to reach the police. *I hope Cazorla figures things out soon.*

39

The Cathedral of Lima, the most important Catholic building in Peru, stands majestic with its two towers and three large doorways in the historic main square known as *Plaza de Armas* along with the Municipal Palace and the Presidential Government Palace.

Bishop Juan Carlos Silvestri stood for a few seconds in front of the tomb of the city founder, Francisco Pizarro. The Spanish conquistador died after being stabbed in the throat in 1541, but his actual remains were not discovered until 1977 and placed into a glass coffin inside the Cathedral for display. Silvestri then walked down the aisles as he contemplated the magnificent works of art. To the left of the main altar, he found the seventeenth-century wooden statue of Saint Augustine.

Thou hast made us for thyself, O Lord, and our heart is restless until it finds its rest in thee. Augustine's quote played in his mind almost like a reflex. It was a good sign, he thought, when he saw a familiar figure approaching him.

"Your excellency," Silvestri said as he leant forward and kissed the Archbishop's gold ring with the traditional violet amethyst.

"Good morning, Father Silvestri. I appreciate you meeting with me today. Please follow me this way."

Silvestri hadn't seen the Archbishop for over a year. Although he might have gained a few pounds, the bearded old priest still looked robust and highly energetic.

In a way the Cathedral was a neutral field. Silvestri would not have been comfortable going to the Archdiocese, where formal audiences would take place. This was a private meeting. No other clergy members were going to be present.

"I love coming to Lima's Cathedral," Silvestri said. "A few years ago, the symphonic orchestra performed Mozart's requiem and it was fantastic. The acoustics of this place are perfect. Maybe we should do those types of concerts more often."

"Maybe we should. This way, please." The Archbishop pointed to the stairs that lead to an underground site right underneath the Major Altar. The sign over the door said *Cripta Arzobispal.* The crypt where Peruvian archbishops have found their final resting place since the mid-1600s.

"Interesting place for a meeting," Silvestri said without hiding some irony in his voice.

"Nobody will interrupt us here. Please have a seat." The Archbishop pointed at a small table with two chairs, in the middle of the room. The walls were white and of a rough unfinished surface with the tombstones of the most distinguished men of the history of the Peruvian Catholic Church. Silvestri thought for a second how ironic it would be, if his endeavor was successful today, the Archbishop would most likely never be buried here.

"Let me tell you, Monsignor, that I have always been a big admirer of yours. You are really a role model for all our priesthood."

"Thank you."

Silvestri knew that the Archbishop would not respond in a welcoming way from the beginning. Still, he continued with his script as planned.

"You know, I think we share a lot of things in common, Father. We both have similar backgrounds. We both were born in Lima, and did our university studies in Spain."

"We have a fundamentally different view on how our government is handling the fight against Shining Path," said the older priest, probably trying not to appear too friendly.

"I think we need to support our government. Defeating terrorism is a complex matter and I would rather leave that to the experts on the field."

"Interesting viewpoint. Did you learn that from Father Josef Andriso?"

Silvestri smiled, trying to hide his surprise. *The old bastard knows about Andriso.* He rested his elbows on the table and placed his hands over his mouth to hide the involuntary lower lip twitch. The old man had obviously done his research. Father Andriso was not really known outside his small academic circle. Maybe he had underestimated him.

"Like I said, we need to be supportive of our government," he said, trying to regain composure, prior to attempting his final argument.

"We cannot close our eyes and choose to ignore flagrant human rights violations."

"Monsignor, everybody is tired of this war that has been going on for years. We both have the same goal. You are the head of the Peruvian Catholic Church. Tell me what I can do to help you, Father. What do you want me to do?"

Silvestri knew that at this point the old priest was going to think he had easily achieved victory.

"For a start, I would like you to publicly express your concerns regarding human rights violations by the armed forces and that you and your order fully support the Archbishop's stance on this matter."

"That shouldn't be a problem, Monsignor."

"Is that right?"

"Absolutely."

"Well then... next, I would..."

"Excuse me for a second, Monsignor."

"What is it?"

"In exchange, I would like to ask you for something. As a sign of good faith."

"What is it?"

"I have a letter with me signed by Cardinal Joseph Ratzinger in which he understands that because of your old age and health concerns..."

"I don't have any health concerns. What are you talking about?"

"...Rome is going to accept your resignation from your extremely stressful position and immediately proceed with the transfer of your services to the Archdiocese of Benevento, where you will continue working as an auxiliary Bishop at the Cattedrale di Santa Maria Assunta."

The Archbishop shook his head in disbelief while still sitting on his chair speechless, as he probably realized that he had been led into a trap.

"And one more thing," Silvestri added. "Armando, the young seminarian that lives in your diocese, should immediately be reassigned to another church."

Villena-Alarcon's face turned red. For a second, he just stayed there without saying anything. Suddenly he got up and slammed his fist on the table violently. "How dare you! You fucking son of a bitch. You and your fucking Opus Dei Mafiosi, you think you can do anything! You need get the fuck out of here now!"

"I'm very sorry I have upset you Monsignor," Silvestri said sincerely. Although he had overpowered his opponent, he had also hoped for a different outcome. "I will leave immediately!"

As he walked out the crypt, he saw the Papal Crest with the Latin inscription *Ut Cognoscant Te*. "That they may know you." Taken from the Gospel of St. John: "And this is eternal life: for men to know You, the only true God, and to know Jesus Christ, whom You have sent."

40

Isabella had just finished presenting her case during rounds and took a step back to allow Dr. Casals to position himself to the right side of the patient's bed. The older man looked thin and debilitated. He had been losing weight for months. Casals listened to his lungs and heart and then pressed on his abdomen gently first and then slightly deeper. "Can you feel this?" he asked Isabella, pointing at the umbilical area. She put her hands and pressed around the belly button. "Yes," she said.

"How would you describe it?"

"It feels like a nodule, rounded and firm."

"It's an umbilical lymph node—it's called the Sister Mary Joseph nodule." He turned his head towards the patient. "Mr. Buendia, I'm going to discuss your case with the members of our team and look at your lab results. We'll come back and talk to you in a few minutes."

"The Sister Mary Joseph lymph node," he told the group walking into the classroom. His voice had a pessimistic tone. "We don't see that very often, but it's almost certain the patient has a malignancy inside the abdomen. The umbilical lymph node is actually a metastatic one. Its presence is almost always a sign of poor prognosis."

"That's really bad for Mr. Buendia," said Guillermo.

"Let's go ahead and order a CT of the abdomen and pelvis."

"Why is it called that? Sister Mary, like a nun?" Isabella asked.

"Sister Mary Joseph was actually an assistant of one of Dr. Mayo's brothers."

"Mayo as in Mayo Clinic?" she asked.

"Correct. She was the one that brought that finding to his attention and later he published it in a medical journal."

"Very cool," said Raul.

"Sometimes nuns do good things," Guillermo said to Isabella, joking.

Casals looked at him a little confused.

"Dr. Casals, Isabella here is a bit of an agnostic," he said in a casual way, trying to be funny.

"Well, that's very interesting, Isabella," he said in an approbatory tone.

"People's response when they hear that is never positive," she said.

"Yes, I know. Most people think that being agnostic or atheist is also being immoral, which is not really true."

"I don't know if I would call myself agnostic. I guess I'm going through a period of skepticism."

"Well, I would be very interested to hear some of your reflections on the subject one of these days. In any case, could please talk to Mr. Buendia and explain what our thoughts are and the test that we're getting." Then turning to the group: "Very well guys, finish your work and for tomorrow why don't you review the management of diabetic ketoacidosis and we can talk about it after rounds."

"Thank you, sir." The medical team could now focus the rest of the day on completing the workup, give updates to patients and families and finish their notes.

"Is he gonna die?" Isabella heard the voice behind her. It was one of the nursing students, wearing an all-light-blue uniform that included the classic nurse cap.

"Hi! What's your name?"

"Carmen, doctor"

"Just call me Isabella, please."

"I've been told to refer to all of you as doctors."

"We're all here to learn. So I don't really care either way." She paused for a second and then she leaned in and whispered. "He probably has advanced cancer and I'm afraid we won't be able to help him."

"That's so sad."

"He doesn't know yet. We need to confirm the diagnosis first."

Carmen had copper skin and dark eyes and her gentle voice had a slight accent of the people from the Andes. Isabella thought she was very pretty by any standards. She wanted to warn her about those horny interns and residents that like to stalk the young, shy nursing students, but Carol interrupted her thoughts. "Mr. Buendia is complaining of pain. Can I give him an extra dose of morphine?"

"Please, Mrs. Carol, go ahead," said Isabella.

"It doesn't look good, right? Some kind of cancer probably?" she asked.

"Yes, and probably an advanced stage, unfortunately. I'm gonna order a CT scan."

She wanted to talk to the new girl, but she saw Guillermo coming her way. "I'll talk to you later, Carmen. Let me know if you have any questions."

"Hey Isabella," he said, as he prompted her to follow him a few steps away. He waited until there was nobody around. "I heard some of the surgery nurses talking about this patient that passed during the night and had a cross painted on the chest."

"Seriously?"

"They were mostly bothered by how mad the surgery attending was, that one of his patients had died at night and nobody could explain how."

"I would like to talk to the nurse that found the body."

"Let's go look for her after lunch. You don't mind if I come with you, right?"

"Not at all. But please don't tell anyone yet."

When she raised her eyes and looked around, she saw Carol looking in her direction. Her face did not appear to show any emotions. Isabella felt a weird, unusual sensation. It took her a few seconds before she realized it was fear.

41

The house was one of those beautiful colonial mansions in downtown Lima known as *casonas*. This one, unfortunately, had been restored and gaudily decorated with loud colors and ostentatious furniture. The picture was somewhat chaotic with multiple agents taking photographs and collecting evidence and police officers coming in and out the multiple rooms. "Let's hurry up, guys! Let's finish this job before the press gets here!" said one of them.

The press! I forgot about them! Probably better if I leave before the press gets here. Father Silvestri found himself rather intrigued by the sight. This was the first time he was present during a crime scene investigation.

"Excuse me, Father?"

The man in front of him appeared to be in his mid-fifties, had dark copper skin and was rather short. He looked extremely familiar; however, the Bishop was not able to remember if he had met him before.

"Good morning, Father Silvestri, I'm captain Raymundo Vidal. I'm with DINCOTE," he said while extending his hand. "Can I ask you a few questions?"

"Of course, Captain Vidal. Nice to meet you." The priest looked around the colorful design of the living room. "Lovely home, wouldn't you say?"

"Not quite my style, Father." The man spoke slowly, with precise words "May I ask you how did you get to be here?"

The Bishop shrugged. "It was just an unusual coincidence. I'm in Lima for a few days." He paused for a second. "Actually, I came for a meeting, *which by the way went horribly bad*, and I'm returning to Ayacucho later this afternoon. I met the victim's family many years ago. His wife asked me to come over and say a prayer for him, which I did. But to be honest, I was also very curious. I've never been to a crime scene before," he said with a smile. "What about you? Why is DINCOTE interested in a crime case?"

"I was not too far from here. I came to see if they needed any help."

"Would it be possible that it's because the victim happened to be a prominent journalist whose opinion articles were not always favorable to the government?"

Vidal's mouth curved slightly upwards as trying to smile politely; however his eyes did not express any feelings.

The priest waited for an answer that never came. "In any case, I'd like to tell you, although I'm not an expert, I believe intelligence is the best way to approach the fight against the terrorists, rather than direct confrontation that leads to multiple casualties, sometimes of innocent people. So, I appreciate what you do."

"Thank you, Father Silvestri."

"I have also heard that the president is not fully supporting your office with appropriate financial resources."

"These are difficult times for everybody, Father, but I definitely appreciate your words."

"May I ask you something, captain?"

Vidal nodded.

"What motivates you to keep searching for Guzman? The man is like a ghost. I can only imagine that after some time it must feel like a very frustrating endeavor."

Vidal's expression did not change.

"Do you know what Shining Path's first violent action in Lima was?" the captain asked.

"I'm not sure I do."

"It happened in 1980. On December 26 , Mao Zedong's birthday. Several stray dogs were found hanging from lamp poles in downtown Lima."

Silvestri could not avoid making a gesture of disgust.

"I love animals, especially dogs. See, Father, I'm a widower. My wife died years ago from leukemia. My daughter is older, already married. It's only me and my dog. An ex-police dog I adopted. A German Shepherd named Pisco. When I saw those animals sacrificed for nothing, I said to myself, one day I'm gonna get this dog killer son of a bitch."

"I see." His answer did not surprise the priest. Silvestri knew people have different motivations in life. "Thank you for sharing that with me."

Vidal nodded in silence.

"By the way, Pisco is a great name for a dog. Anyway, I should probably go. Let me know if I can be of any help in your future endeavors, captain."

"I will definitely keep you in mind, Father Silvestri."

"And just in case, can I have your direct phone number? In case it happens that I learn of any new information that could help your investigations?"

42

"Psychopathy is a personality disorder characterized by an abnormal lack of empathy, lack of emotional response, in other words lack of compassion for other humans." The professor spoke slowly, emphasizing every single word as he walked back and forth in front of the class. "Psychopathy is also often associated with amoral behavior and no feelings of guilt." Isabella remembered that day very well. She found the subject of personality disorders the most fascinating subject in all of psychiatry. The attending was wearing the classic attire for most medicine professors those days: a wrinkly white coat on top of his white dress shirt and navy-blue dress pants. She remembered looking around at her classmates. Among the other sixty-four students that were brilliant or lucky enough to make it all the way to this point, she could detect all kinds of personality disorder traits: histrionic, narcissistic, passive-aggressive and probably most of them had something of an obsessive-compulsive behavior. During their first year, there was this extremely reserved and solitary guy, that in retrospect probably had a schizoid type personality. He ended up developing full schizophrenia and unfortunately had to quit school a year later. *Crazy Ricky. I wonder how he's doing these days?*

"Psychopaths do not experience shame or remorse for their actions. The classic psychopath is the criminal. But not all psychopaths are criminals. Your very charming friend from high school, your neighbor, maybe the guy sitting next to you, could be one." Everybody looked at each other laughing.

"Okay guys, that's all for today. Tomorrow in our practice session, we'll be analyzing the movie "One Flew Over the Cuckoo's Nest" from 1975. Have a nice evening, gentlemen!"

And now, one year later, she was probably in front of a real psychopathic character. A really dangerous one.

"I don't remember her age exactly, but probably late sixties" said the nurse in green scrubs. "Had a perforated bowel. Required multiple trips to the OR. Issues with wound infections. One of those complicated postop cases that any surgeon would hate."

"Was she in a lot of pain?" Isabella asked

"Yes. Severe pain."

"Would you say she was suffering?"

"Yeah, I'd say so. She was in a lot of pain. Multiple drains. She had a terrible-looking open abdominal wound."

"What do you guys think she died from?" Guillermo asked.

"Probably from sepsis, wound infection for sure."

"And you said there was a drawing on her chest. Can you describe it?"

"Yeah, it was a little cross just below the left clavicle. First I thought maybe it was a tattoo, but it looks like it was made with a marker."

"This may sound weird, but any particular type of cross?"

"Actually, this one had a sort of a loop in the upper bar."

Isabella drew the cross she had seen before on a piece of paper. "Like this?"

"Yep. Just like that one. Any other questions? I've got to go back to the post-surgery area."

"No. No more questions. Thank you."

Isabella stared at the wall for a few seconds.

"Something wrong?" Guillermo wondered.

"Let's go. There is something I never mentioned to anybody before," said Isabella, as they left the surgical ward. "The cross that I saw was a particular type. The so-called Egyptian cross, with a loop in the upper bar."

"What does that mean?"

"Meaning it cannot all be a coincidence. It's the same person behind all these patients' deaths."

"Like a serial killer?"

She did not reply right away.

"Is everything okay?

"Let me think." She took a deep breath and after a few seconds started writing on a piece of paper as they sat down in one of the benches. "This is the first time that I can say with certainty that something really wrong is happening here."

"Looks like you were right this whole time."

"As far as we know there have been three dead patients with a sign of a cross drawn somewhere in the upper body. At least in one case that I was directly involved with the care, the patient died in somewhat obscure circumstances. All three cases were over sixty. The first one, I remember, was extremely malnourished, chronically ill and probably suffering. The last case, the one that we just learned about, was in terrible pain. Mrs. Jimenez, however, does not fit very well that actively dying, suffering patient, although she was old and did have episodes of severe leg pain."

"Who would be interested in killing those people?"

"I've been reading about different types of criminals and murderers and I've found something called angels of mercy. A type of serial killer, usually a caregiver, like a nurse, most commonly a woman that kills the victim in order to prevent any further suffering."

"So, our main suspect right now would be one of the hospital nurses."

"I think so. We need to get the schedule of all the hospital nurses and see who was working those days. Since at least two of the deaths happened during the night, I would be more suspicious of night-shift nurses."

"And how are we gonna get the schedules? Maybe Mrs. Carol can help us."

"No, I'd rather not ask her, she acted a little weird when I told her about the black cross on Mrs. Jimenez' face."

"So, what then?"

"I don't know. Asking for the schedule to the nursing director is going to sound extremely unusual. I may have to sneak into her office."

"I hope you can find a different way. You don't want to get in any more trouble. Carlos is friend with the surgical nurses; he may be able to get you the surgery nurses' schedules."

"That would be nice but, how to ask without raising some suspicion?"

"Should we talk to Casals again, or maybe Dr. Cazorla, the Dean?"

"I don't even know who to trust and who not to. What if one of the doctors is involved? Like one of the residents or attending physicians?"

"A psychopath serial killer doctor? You are not serious. We are doctors, we don't kill people."

"You honestly believed most of these guys have noble ideals in mind, right? You are a nice, honest guy, Guillermo. Maybe I was that way too, but after a few bad experiences in life, it's hard for me to trust anybody. "

"Don't be so negative!"

"I think you are a little bit like Casals, in love with the old school academic approach to medicine, but I don't think all the doctors share this idealistic version. Many physicians choose this field because it's a prestigious and well-paid career. Why did you go into medicine?"

"Medicine was always appealing to me because it involves applying scientific knowledge in a practical way to help other people. But I've got to be honest. There is also the money factor. I said it. Being a doctor is going to open doors for a lot more opportunities in society, or at least that's what I hope. I don't like to be poor."

"You aren't poor. There are a lot of poor people in this country and you are not one of them."

"You're talking of extreme poverty. That's definitely not me. I don't know, maybe it's hard to understand for you, Isabella. Don't take it in the wrong way, please, but your family is rich. You grew up with everything available. My case is a little different. There were periods of time when my Dad was unemployed, and days when we didn't have anything to eat at home. I don't want my future family to have to go through that. I don't want to be like my Dad, agonizing with that uncertainty of not knowing how you are going to feed your children the next day."

"I'm sorry to hear that." Isabella looked down, not knowing what else to say.

"It's okay. Sorry, I should not assume that because your family has money that you have everything you need."

She nodded.

"What are you doing later? Some of the guys are gonna stop by *El Hueco* for a beer before going home. Do you wanna join us?" He was hoping she would say yes.

"No, thank you. I need to find out what nurses were working those days that the killings happened. I need to find a way to get copies of their schedules for the last few months."

"It sounds like you're obsessing a little bit too much about the whole thing. Please do not get in more trouble."

43

Like every evening, Monsignor Villena- Alarcon waited impatiently for the 8 p.m. news. He had not heard anything about Silvestri for the last few days. The meeting could have not been worse, and he needed time to think how to prevent the whole situation from turning into a mess. He started to wonder if maybe it was time to resign. He could ask the Jesuit leaders to be reassigned to another country. Spain would be nice. A smaller city near the coast, maybe.

"Excuse me, Monsignor," said Armando. "Would you like me to bring your dinner here?"

"Yes, my dear Armando. Here will be just fine. You know I love to watch the news."

The food is not as good as it used to be. I wonder if they got a new cook. Monsignor got distracted just for a second before redirecting his attention on the TV set. The news again described a new terrorist attack just outside Lima.

"I do not want to condone terrorism, Armando. We need to defeat the Shining Path. You know this has become an obsession of mine. However, the government still does not have a plan to solve the root of the problem. And the root of the problem, my dear Armando, is not only the extreme poverty that millions of Peruvians have to live with every day but also the extreme degree of inequality. When the wealth and the power concentrate in a very small percentage of the population, the result is social instability, and social instability leads to revolutions."

"You said 'revolutions,' Father?" Armando's face had a frightened expression.

"I did. But you don't have to worry about it, my dear friend. We are safe here. Nobody messes around with the Catholic Church, not even the terrorists. But I think I talked too much already. Tell me, Armando, how was your day today?"

"Very good, Father. I visited Saint Toribio's orphanage with Father Pedro. We helped the nuns clean the entire place."

"Excellent! It's so nice to hear how much you are helping our communities. But you must be exhausted. Here, why don't you sit down right here next to me," Monsignor said, as he noticed his own heartbeat accelerating from the anticipation. "I'm going to finish this dinner and then I'm going to give you a massage. One of those full-body massages that you like so much."

44

"Look who is here to see you, Isabella, your good friend Andrea!" Isabella's Mother said. It was actually a nice surprise to have an unanticipated visit after a long day at work.

"I'm gonna let you hang out, girls. There is some food in the fridge if you are hungry."

"Thank you, Mrs. Castle."

Isabella left the car keys on the kitchen table and took her coat off. "Wow, kind of unexpected."

"Sometimes you have to do unexpected things," Andrea said with a smile.

"Hungry? Something to eat?"

"Not really hungry."

"Something to drink maybe?"

"Do you have soda? Coca Cola maybe?"

"What about a beer?"

Andrea's eyes widened.

"Or even better, I'll make you a rum and coke."

"Does your mommy let you drink alcohol at home?"

"Ha! Very funny. Let me show you how to make a decent Cuba Libre. I'll be back in a second with a good Jamaican rum."

"Okay," she said with a half-smile.

A minute later, Isabella was back with a bottle and two glasses.

"Lots of ice. Then fill a third of the glass with rum. Fill the rest with Coke. Preferably not Diet Coke. And a slice of lime. And voila!" Isabella raised a glass. "A perfect Cuba Libre for my friend Andrea!"

"Let's have a toast."

"Okay."

"To our friendship!"

"That's so cliché!" Isabella gave a little giggle. "What about a toast for Ricky?"

"Ricky? Ricky who?"

"Remember Ricky? Our corpse in anatomy class?" Isabella could not stop laughing.

"Oh my God, Ricky! Of course, I remember! Cheers!"

"Let's go to the living room so I can put on some music."

"Sounds good."

As they both walked into the living room, Isabella realized this was a part of the house she had not been to in a long time. She had almost forgotten how comfortable these modern leather couches were.

"Not too loud or my Mom will get hysterical," she said while inserting one of her cassette tapes on the stereo system.

"This is so good," Andrea said as she sipped on her rum and coke. "What's your worst memory of medical school?"

"That's kind of an odd question. The OB/GYN rotation. No question."

"I didn't like that one either. Too many vaginas. Not cute vaginas. Ugly, hairy vaginas, vaginas with malodorous, cottage cheese discharges, and vaginas dry and wrinkly that have not been used in years." She laughed.

"Oh my God, you're so funny. My case was different."

"Because you like vaginas?" She giggled.

"You're funny! For the record, I'm not into vaginas, okay?" Isabella felt she needed to clarify. Andrea could have easily heard those lesbian rumors in the hospital. Then she paused for a second, thinking. "Let's just say the environment was not very welcoming for female students."

"Can you explain a little more?"

"I was the only female on the team. I had to deal with inappropriate comments and jokes all the time. I felt I was continuously harassed by the residents and the attending would suddenly appear behind me massaging my neck and shoulders, saying, "Honey, you look a little tense.""

Andrea was listening with a disgusted face. "I'm really sorry to hear that. My rotation wasn't bad. The attending physician was a woman."

"That's why I don't have very good memories. But it's okay.

"What do you like the best so far?"

"I like this medicine rotation. You know why? I'm finally using my new stethoscope, that my Dad bought following my very specific instructions: "Red Littman Master Cardiology II.""

"Oh, so fancy! I have the Classic II that most people have."

"You know, I was a little OCD preparing for junior intern year, I knew it was going to be mentally and physically demanding so I even planned what type of clothes I was gonna wear."

"That sounds like a full obsessive-compulsive."

"I know, right? I also didn't want to look very girly, so most of my clothes are in a range of dark colors from dark blue to light gray or black, which will also help me to look tougher and more decisive."

"Now it sounds just like plain insecurity to me." She shrugged.

"I even thought about how to wear the stethoscope. Yeah, if you wear it hanging straight down holding from the back of the neck, makes you look like an old doctor, it's not cool. Instead you should wear the stethoscope around the neck, way much cooler."

"Please, keep going, you're making me laugh!"

"It took me a long time to decide what type of fanny pack I wanted. Yes, the fanny pack is an indispensable tool for the interns."

"Totally agree. Where else can you carry a flashlight, tape measure, syringes and tubes for blood draws, epinephrine and atropine amps ready to use for cardiac arrest?"

"Every student and intern wears one. But I wanted something more unique. I found a cool black leather one from a street vendor downtown."

"Oh my god! You know you are spoiled, right?"

"I've gone through some challenging times, too." Isabella raised her empty glass. "Ready for a second round?"

"Let's do it."

"What's the name of this song? I really like it," Andrea asked as she started to sing along the music.

"It's called 'Pure' by a band named the Lightning Seeds."

"I'm gonna have to remember that."

45

Guillermo could easily identify the delicious smell of his Mother's *arroz con pollo* from outside the apartment.

"Good, you're here already," his Mother said as soon as he opened the door. "Go wash your hands and sit at the table to eat. Dinner's gonna get cold."

"Mom, I just got home."

"I'm telling you, dinner's gonna get cold. Go and wash your hands. This needs a little more salt," she said, adding seasoning to the food.

Guillermo's Dad was sitting at the kitchen table, enjoying the show. "You guys should have your own sitcom."

"Very funny! You're gonna wash the dishes tonight!" she said, laughing.

"How was the hospital, son?"

My Dad has perfected the art of knowing how to quickly change the topic.

"Very well, Dad. It's been a good month so far. And where is my sister?"

"She's gonna stay at her friend Paula's tonight, which, just between you and me, is kind of nice. We all need a break from hysterical high-school girls sometimes."

"I can see Mom is in a great mood. Anything going on?"

"Your Dad was offered a new job. Tell him, honey."

"It's not a big deal."

"Come on, Dad, I'd like to know."

"My friend Alex asked me to join his company in a manager position."

"And it pays a lot more than where your Dad is right now."

"That's great, Dad!" The first thought that immediately came to Guillermo's mind was that, maybe soon, he could have a car. It didn't have to be new or fancy. Just a car so he didn't have to ride the bus anymore. *That would be a dream.*

"I don't know, guys, I think I'm doing okay in my current job. This new position would likely involve traveling out of town often and likely working some weekends."

"Well, I guess, that's why they pay more, right honey?" his Mother said. "And doesn't it have more potential for growth in the future?"

"I guess that's true, but who wants to work more? Right? I'd rather stay at home and hang out with my wife and kids. Not to mention that with the current climate of instability in the country, maybe it's better to stay at your safe, old job."

Guillermo was not surprised to hear that. His Dad's attitude was not new. Always reluctant to change, either too fearful to take any risks or too lazy to try harder. He chose to think it was the first one. He looked around the small apartment. All the furniture was more than twenty years old. The carpets needed to be replaced a long time ago, especially since their twelve-year-old cat started to have incontinence issues.

He shook his head and looked down with disappointment.

"And you know what else? Guillermo is gonna finish medical school very soon. He'll be working as a doctor and will be making pretty good money. We may even be able to move to a bigger place!"

I guess I won't be getting my own car any time soon.

46

Andrea grabbed her third glass of rum and coke, walked around the living room and stopped in front of the painting of an archangel holding an arquebus.

"The Cusco school of painting," Isabella said. "Do you like it?"

"It's beautiful. Is it original? Like eighteenth century original?"

"I actually don't know, but that's very possible. I'd have to ask my Dad. I remember when I was a little girl, I used to ask the adults, "How is it that an angel is carrying a firearm?""

"And what did they say?"

"I can't remember. Probably something not very smart."

"I wanted to ask you…" Andrea hesitated for a second. "Why did we stop seeing each other?"

"Why? You don't know? I was resentful."

"Resentful! I never realized. Why?"

"When Arturo and I broke up, it didn't take too long for him to find another girlfriend, that Patty whore, and you continued being nice to him. I felt like you betrayed me. You were my friend first."

"I see. I'm sorry. If it helps I never really liked Patty and I don't talk to him anymore."

"It's okay. I'm over it. We don't need to talk about it."

"So, are you dating anyone now?"

"I just wanna be single for a while." She poured more ice into her glass. "What about you?"

"No, no really. Carlos suggested I go out with Freddy Revilla once. Freddy is a nice guy, a little quiet. Not really my type. But you know what, now that I'm thinking, you may actually like him. You are both a little bit antisocial," she said with a chuckle. "And he is really into music just like you."

"He actually rescued me at El Hueco the other day. Hugo was being a total dick."

"Hugo, he's such a pervert!"

"He's my resident, unfortunately."

"Freddy must like you, then. Let me look into that. I'll ask Carlos."

"Please no, Andrea. I already have too many things going on."

At that moment the front door opened. It was Isabella's Father.

"Hi girls!" he said as he walked in the living room. He was wearing a navy-blue blazer and dark gray dress pants. With his tanned complexion and a big confident smile, most people found Mr. Castle extremely charming. "Andrea, it's nice to see you, it's been a while."

"Hi baby." He kissed Isabella on the forehead.

"Well, it looks like you're having a good time," he said, noticing the drinks on the coffee table. "I'll go say hi to your Mom."

Andrea waited for a few seconds and then with a complicit smile she whispered, "Your Dad is so handsome!"

"I haven't been very fond of him lately."

"What's wrong?"

"I barely see him. He's never home. Some rumors say that he's cheating on my Mom."

"What! Wait, are you sure or only rumors? Who says that?"

"My cousin told me that her Mom mentioned something about it."

"That doesn't sound like a strong confirmation of facts."

"I am also resentful because I'm afraid he's one of the reasons my brother left."

"How so?"

"Let's not talk about that today."

"I have a question."

"Oh no."

"No worries. It's a different topic. You said that you chose your clothes in order to look tougher and more decisive. I don't really understand why you would need to do that. You're super smart. You've always been a very good student."

"For the entire time I've been in medical school I've felt that because I'm a woman I have to work harder sometimes and restrain myself some other times in order to be able to compete with men. I want to show everybody that I'm a very good doctor."

"So, in other words, you are looking for external validation?"

"External validation? Yeah, that's possible. I just want to show those fuckers that I'm better than them."

"Isabella, when did you start swearing so much?"

"Since I started going to therapy, I guess. It's liberating. You should try it sometime."

47

Silvestri looked around one more time to be sure nobody at the diocese of Ayacucho was nearby. It would have been highly unusual to be on the phone this late at night.

"Father Andriso, Can you hear me well?"

"Good morning, son…or good night? What's the time there?"

"It's almost four in the morning, Father."

"I'm so sorry. I always forget the time difference."

"That's not a problem for me. I've been waiting to hear from you. As you know, my meeting with the Archbishop didn't go very well."

"I know, my dear Juan Carlos. It's really unfortunate to hear. Anyway, this is going to be a very short call. We had a long meeting this morning. It was actually kind of exhausting. Mostly everybody pretty much agreed to give you a green light to move forward as you had recommended. Your particular approach to this kind of problem has always been highly effective." He paused, maybe looking for the right words. "What I'm trying to say is that we trust your judgment and your methods to secure direct government collaboration. We all know you for many years now and are very proud of you. You are the future of our order. God Bless you, my son!"

"Thank you, Father Andriso. I've already initiated the talks with the people that are going to help us and so far, everything is moving in the right direction."

"One more thing, and I hate to say this. If somehow the plan fails and your name is brought up publicly, our order and Rome will not be standing behind you."

"I'm very aware of that, Father Andriso."

Bishop Juan Carlos Silvestri hung up the phone. He sat there for interminable minutes staring at the wall in silence. After so many years the same phrase still resonated in his head:

Our mission is to protect our church. We must be champions of our faith.

"At all costs."

48

It took a few weeks from the beginning of the medicine rotation for Isabella to feel confident that she was efficient at her work. She had developed a daily morning routine: first she took a quick walk around the unit to be sure none of her patients were actively decompensating. She checked with the nurses to see if there were any overnight problems that needed to be addressed right away, like very high blood pressure or a severe electrolyte deficiency. After that, she reviewed the morning labs or any notes left by the consultants on the case. In any event, she was always the first one of the medical team to be in the unit and not infrequently the last one to leave. Although she had almost finished all her assessments, it was still early so she was a little surprised to see Casals walking in the ward that morning.

"Good morning Isabella!"

"Good morning, Dr. Casals."

"Did you check on all your patients already?"

"For the most part, yes, sir."

"I'm gonna get a coffee before we start rounds. Why don't you walk with me and we continue our conversation from the other day?"

She hesitated for a second. "Do you want me to tell you my thoughts about religion?"

"Would that be okay?"

"I'd love that, sir."

"Okay, let's go."

"Sir, I just want to be sure that what I share with you isn't going to affect how you grade my performance on this rotation," she said as they left the medical ward.

"Of course not," he said laughing.

His response was reassuring. It was unusual to find somebody to talk about her feelings on that subject without having to play defense. But she felt Casals was different.

"I'm not sure where to start. One of my first thoughts on this matter is that there are many religions and which one you practice strongly correlates with the part of the world you live in. For example, if I'd been born in the Middle East, I would not have grown up Catholic. My parents would be Muslim and I would probably be Muslim too. So, if Christians accept that I must believe in Jesus in order to go to heaven, then I would go to hell simply because of geographic reasons. I do not think that is a fair system designed by God."

"Like a geographic curse." Casals smiled.

"Exactly." She began to feel more comfortable talking. "Every year thousands of little kids, let's say under age five, die unbaptized in developing countries in Africa and Asia. Most of them did not grow up in Christian families. They never heard or knew about Jesus. Are they supposed to go to hell? The catechism says that baptism is needed for salvation. It would be extremely cruel for God to allow these kids to be born only to be sent to hell a few years later. Why punish them? That's not consistent with the all loving God we were taught."

Casals nodded in agreement. "In the Roman Catholic tradition, unbaptized babies go to Limbo after death."

"I heard that. For how long? Do they stay there? They're innocent beings, why can't they go to heaven? I have asked this type of question to more than one priest and the answer always is "we don't really understand God's plan, it's a mystery but there must be a good reason why these things happened." I've never been satisfied with these answers. I'm so confused. What do you think?"

"It's simple, Isabella," he said calmly as he grabbed a cup of coffee. "Would you like a coffee, too?"

"No, sir. Thank you."

"You're able to analyze things in a rational and critical way. That's how your brain works. Most people's intellects don't work that way. They never question what they are told. Unfortunately, you won't be able to explain religion that way. You're asking for rational explanations and logical correlations like in science. In other words, you're asking for evidence. Faith is to believe without evidence."

"I'm not sure I understand."

"Everything that you said is entirely rational. Your questions are absolutely reasonable. I'm afraid they won't help you to explain religion."

"Should I just believe without asking questions?"

"That's your choice. But if you choose not to believe, don't feel guilty about it. That'd be my advice."

"It's hard for me not to be skeptical when things don't make sense."

"A certain dose of skepticism is always good and will be very valuable for you, especially in the future."

"How is that?"

"In a few years from now, Internet use will become ubiquitous, faster and easier. We'll be able to access an enormous amount of information in a matter of seconds. You will be able to find medical journals and write your research article from home."

"I can't wait for that."

"But at the same time, posting information online will also be easier. I can see ill-intentioned people posting all kinds of misinformation just to manipulate public opinion."

49

"Did you hear Casals the other day? Occam's razor?!" Guillermo shook his head in disbelief. "He keeps surprising me every time. Before this rotation, I thought my knowledge of history and other general stuff was very good, but this guy continues to amaze me. He's at a totally different level."

"I actually went and read about William of Occam," said Isabella.

"Oh good, reading something not related to medicine or serial killers," he joked. "Did you learn something worth mentioning?"

"Yes, he was actually a Franciscan priest. The Catholic Church did not like the Franciscan idea of the church having to stay poor, and he was excommunicated."

"You're always looking for bad things to say about religion!"

She raised both arms. "I'm sorry, it's not intentional, I swear."

"Hey, let's go get some lunch."

"I actually brought some food from home. My Mom's *lomo saltado* is excellent."

"Well, let me show you another place where you can eat lunch with a little more privacy. So you don't walk into Igor from the morgue. Let's walk this way."

"Where are we going?"

"The residents call rooms buildings. There is a lounge with a dining table and chairs and most of the time nobody goes there. Sometimes I go there to read."

"Sounds good."

"So, what happened the other day? Did you get access to the nurses' schedules?"

"Yes, it was not difficult at all. I asked Carmen, the cute nursing student, to help me. I suggested a research study for her regarding working night shifts and risk factors for nurse burnout. We needed to see how many shifts on average every nurse worked. So, she formally requested the nurse's schedules for her project and now I have them."

"You are so freaking smart!"

"So, I got copies of every night shift for the last few months. I went through these schedules over the weekend. It was a lot of work. I have the names of the nurses that were working the same nights that the last two patients were murdered."

"You mean the same night the patients died? You still don't have enough evidence to say there were murdered."

She ignored that comment "One of those nurses was Mrs. Carol, our unit head nurse."

"Holy crap!"

"Now, I'm starting to think there must be a reason why Carol was so uncomfortable when I mentioned the cross drawn on Mrs. Jimenez' face."

"So, you think she's an angel of mercy. Wow! It's kind of makes sense."

"And now I'm afraid she's gonna kill Mr. Buendia. She was listening carefully during rounds. She knows he probably has advanced cancer. Mr. Buendia fills the victim's profile for an angel of mercy killer: an old patient with a terminal illness."

"The victim's profile? You are talking like a movie detective now."

As they walked inside the residents building, Guillermo was ready to ask what she was going to do with the information when they saw Carlos and Freddy sitting at the table. At first impression, it appeared they were having an argument about something serious.

"I'm telling you," Freddy said, "I did a lot of research for a project in high school."

"A high-school project on the history of heavy metal?"

"Yes. We were told to write an essay about something that we were passionate about. And I did a lot of research and listened to a lot of songs of bands that I never heard about."

"Hey guys," Carlos said. "Come and join us, I would like you to hear Freddy talking about the origins of heavy metal."

"That sounds pretty interesting," Guillermo said

"While Black Sabbath's first album is considered the very first heavy metal album, there is no consensus on the very first heavy metal song. But in my opinion, I'll give that honor to a band named Iron Butterfly. The name of the song was "In a Gadda Da Vida," and has a really psychedelic gloomy guitar riff."

"In a gadda what? I've never heard about it." Carlos looked unconvinced.

"What about Cream's 'Sunshine of Your Love.' That's a very heavy riff." Guillermo asked.

"That's true. It's also in this period they call proto-metal. But 'In a Gadda Da Vida' has more distorted guitar and the feeling of imminent doom, closer to early Sabbath's."

"That's fancy music critic talking right there," Carlos said with a sarcastic voice.

"Hey Isabella," said Guillermo. "This guy here knows a lot about music. He might be able to challenge you."

"I really doubt it," she said with a shy smile.

But Freddy did not appear willing to engage in a competition. "It's nothing," he said.

"Do you know the very first punk rock song?" she asked.

"First punk rock song ever? I'd imagine something by the Ramones or Sex Pistols," Freddy said.

"You guys know?" she asked the whole group now.

They shook their heads.

"Punk music didn't really emerge until the mid-seventies, right? However, if you listen to Los Saicos' 'Demolición' from 1964, you will notice it has all the elements of punk rock. Some pundits say this was the original punk song."

"Really? Los Saicos? Never heard of them. Where are they from?" Guillermo asked.

"From Peru."

"No fucking way!" Carlos said.

The three interns looked at each other. They'd just been schooled on the history of rock music by a girl.

50

Bishop Silvestri felt relieved to be back in Ayacucho. Local matters were always much more simple and easier to handle. Despite growing up in the capital city, Lima had become too chaotic for him. He had just stepped outside the Diocese and was ready to light a cigarette when a powerful voice with a Spanish accent interrupted his thoughts.

"How was your trip to Lima, Father Silvestri?"

"Father Pablo! It's nice to see you. It didn't go as well as I would've wanted. But nothing unexpected. Sometimes I feel that Lima doesn't welcome me anymore. I can almost feel its hostility. I'm not sure I'll be able to live back there again."

"I understand what you're saying. After more than twenty years living here, I don't think I could live in a city like Madrid anymore."

"Something interesting happened in Lima, though. I had the chance to be at a crime scene investigation."

"Oh, my Lord! What happened?"

"A local journalist was found dead at his home and the family, who I've known for many years, asked me to go and say a prayer for him."

"I see. Was it difficult to pray while looking at the victim?"

"It was horrifying. Anyway, while in there I met Captain Raymundo Vidal."

"I don't think I recognize that name"

"He's a policeman with DINCOTE. They investigate terrorism-related activities. What was he doing at a police crime investigation?"

"I couldn't tell, Juan Carlos. I'm not sure what you are trying to tell me."

"Well, I don't think this crime was perpetrated by terrorists since the victim was actually very critical of the brutal response of the government in the form of paramilitary activity."

"So…you are saying…"

"Vidal's presence there makes me think he feels one of these paramilitary groups could be behind the journalist's death."

"I don't know much about politics but I do know some people in our church are not happy about how you have not openly criticized the government for this type of action."

"I know, Father Pablo, and I may need to be more careful in the future. However, I do have a major problem to deal with and I do need the full collaboration of the government."

"I'm much older than you, son, and the only thing I would suggest is to pray to our lord for guidance and follow his advice."

"Thank you, Father, of course I will."

"I'll see you inside later."

"I'm just gonna finish my cigarette," he said as he flicked the ashes into the ground.

As he watched Father Pablo returning inside, he took a deep puff and then exhaled slowly with pleasure as he contemplated the stunning clear blue sky and the snow-capped mountain range of the Andes.

We must protect our church.

51

Isabella looked at the clock on the wall anxiously. It was time to leave.

Rounds had gone well, uneventfully like had been the case lately. Having Casals as an attending was a little overwhelming at first, and the initial weeks had been very mentally taxing, but now as she was getting more comfortable with the routine work she was also trying to enjoy the process.

"What would you do in this case? Your lab results are not gonna be back for a few days," asked Casals.

"Everything points to a case of an acute autoimmune condition, since there is no obvious infection and all our cultures are negative. I think we should start treatment with high-dose steroids right away."

"That's right. I don't disagree with you, Hugo. However, you should explain to the patient that diagnosis still is not final and that treatment with high-dose corticosteroids can have serious side effects."

Hugo, the only resident on the team, also appeared more relaxed and his interventions were more accurate and more valuable for the group. Maybe even his demeanor was more pleasant. *Maybe he is not that bad after all.*

"What are you gonna do after you finish your residency, Hugo?" Casals asked.

"I'm gonna go back to my hometown of Cajamarca."

"Why are you not staying in Lima?" asked Guillermo.

"There is too much competition here. Everybody wants to practice in the big capital city. Cajamarca is very nice. There are a lot of opportunities for general practitioners. Weather is nice and terrorism has not had a major presence. At least not yet. My Dad owns a retail business and my uncle was a major a few years back. Definitely have some family connections, so establishing a new practice shouldn't be too hard."

"That sounds like a really good plan," Isabella said. Since the day of the lunch at *El Hueco*, she had tried to maintain a safe distance from Hugo and keep their relationship strictly work-related.

"The market in Lima is very saturated. There are too many doctors and not enough patients with money to pay for their services. Most people don't have health insurance. The private hospitals take advantage of this situation. Some of my friends are getting paid five dollars per hour to be the in-house hospital doctor."

"Five dollars per hour! That's so low!" Guillermo said. He looked disappointed.

"Sounds like you have a good plan. Very good luck with that, Hugo." Casals never missed an opportunity to show support to his students. "Let me know if there is anything I can do to help."

"Thank you, sir"

"Okay. Good work guys. Don't forget to read about antibiotics for gram-negative infections. See you tomorrow."

As the group dispersed, Isabella walked towards Guillermo.

"You look upset. Something wrong?"

"Five dollars per hour! I guess what kind of future can I have that way? Wait until I tell my Dad, he'll be disappointed for sure."

"Your Dad?"

"Yes, he's expecting me to help support the family when I'm finished with school."

"I'm sorry." She tried to say something nice but she was not particularly good at it.

"Hey, I wanted to ask you, how do you know so much about music?"

"My older brother was a huge influence, I guess. I grew up listening to a lot of his records. What about you? You know a lot about music too."

"I never told you before, but my high school friend had a band and I used to hang out with them all the time. I was planning on being their producer. It was a fun time."

"And then you decided to become a doctor."

"I guess." His voice was still disheartened.

She wished she could talk to him a little longer. "Hey, I need to leave for about an hour, okay?"

"Where are you going?"

"I have an appointment with Dr. Cazorla at 11 a.m. I'm going to show him all the information I've gathered about this angel of mercy case and ask him to contact the police."

"Okay. I hope the meeting goes well."

"There are some pending lab results for bed 5; could you please check on those?

"Absolutely."

As Isabella left her unit, a familiar face was sitting on the bench outside.

"Hey Isabella!"

"How is it going? She was surprised to see Freddy far from the surgery ward.

"It's going well," he said. He paused awkwardly for a few seconds.

Was he waiting for me?

"I was wondering if you would wanna come to the movies with me sometime?"

The question took Isabella completely by surprise. She raised her eyebrows and took a deep breath. *Did he just ask me to go out on a date?*

"Anything good at the movie theaters these days?" she replied while still trying to process the question.

52

Isabella looked around the nicely decorated Dean's office and approved the good taste. On the desk there was a professionally taken picture of the Dean with his wife and daughters.

"Thank you for having me, Dr. Cazorla. You have a beautiful family, by the way." Her time with the psychologist had also taught her techniques of how to better interact with people, something that did not come to her naturally.

"Thank you. And thank you for coming. I love being able to talk directly with our students, learn how things are going and help with whatever problem they have. You're doing your medicine rotation with Dr. Casals, correct?"

"Yes, Dr. Cazorla."

"How are things going? Are you having a positive experience?"

"Yes, Dr. Cazorla. I love working with Dr. Casals."

"I'm happy to hear that. Dr. Casals is one of our best teachers. That's why getting the rotation is so competitive. Consider yourself very lucky. Well, tell me how I can help you today."

"I know that what I'm going to say is going to sound strange, but please hang in there with me while I'm telling you."

"I'm listening," he said, leaning forward.

"I have witnessed the death of three patients in weird circumstances that make me believe that somebody was actually trying to hurt them."

"I'm sorry, I'm not following."

"I think somebody may have killed these three patients."

Cazorla's friendly smile slowly disappeared. He placed his elbows on the desk to let his chin rest in between his hands. His eyes narrowed down.

"Okay, and what makes you believe that?"

"The three of them had drawn a black Egyptian cross, either in the chest or on the face."

"Egyptian cross?"

"Yes. It looks like this," she said as she quickly drew the cross with the loop on top.

"Does this Egyptian cross have any specific meaning?"

"It's also known as Ankh. It's an ancient Egyptian hieroglyph that means 'life.' The circle on the top means that there is no beginning or no end. So, it could also be interpreted as a symbol for immortality."

"Was the murderer trying to communicate something?"

"That I don't know. Maybe he thought that person's death was the beginning of a new life without pain or suffering and he was facilitating that transition."

"And the patients have one of these drawn on their face?"

"Yes sir, actually my very own patient, Mrs. Jimenez, had a cross painted on her left cheek. The other two patients each had one drawn on their chest."

"Very interesting. Looks like you have been doing a lot of research. What else have you learned?"

"All these three patients were older and in one way or another experiencing pain. I believe that the person that did it was acting to relieve their suffering. I have read of a particular type of serial killer called angels of mercy. And because more commonly these angels of mercy happened to be a caregiver or a nurse, I suspected first that it could be a nurse. I obtained the nursing night schedules and I looked at who was working when these patients died, and I found four nurses that worked on both night shifts."

"How did you get those schedules?"

"That's not really important, sir, I think these women should be suspects and should probably be interrogated by the police."

"The police?"

"Yes, I was hoping that you would contact the police and share with them the results of my investigation. I don't think I can prove anything by myself. In order to move forward I think we'll need help from the police. I'm also particularly wary of Miss Carol from my medical floor."

"Miss Carol, the old charge nurse? But she doesn't work the night shift."

"Apparently she does occasionally in order to bring more money home, and she did work on both nights. However, when I casually mentioned the cross on Mrs. Jimenez' face, she started acting somewhat suspicious. She may know or may have seen something. Or maybe there is more than one killer, working as a team."

"Now, I'm really impressed. What you are telling me is really fascinating. I've never seen anything like this in all these years that I've been a doctor."

Isabella wasn't sure if the man in front of him was serious or just making fun of her.

"Would it be possible for me to keep these nursing schedules?" he asked.

"Of course. I also have an article about angels of mercy serial killers. Would you want an extra copy, sir?"

"Absolutely."

"Well, that's all I have to say."

"Let me ask you one more thing, Isabella. Have you talked to anybody regarding this?"

"I did mention it to Dr. Casas after I saw my patient Mrs. Jimenez. I never told him about the third case."

"Anybody else?"

"No. Nobody else."

"Thank you very much, Isabella. I will get in touch with the police immediately."

"Thank you, sir."

"Do me a favor, please. Do not talk to anybody about this, okay?"

53

"Dr. Casals, are you leaving soon?" asked Guillermo. It was not unusual for Casals to stay after rounds, reviewing the clinical notes and in general making himself available for questions and problems that could arise.

"In another thirty minutes probably. I have an early clinic today," he said while reading a patient's chart.

"Can I ask you a question?"

"Of course. How can I help?"

"I guess I'm just concerned about the future, sir. I'm afraid I may have to emigrate to another country."

"I can assure my friend that you're not the only one having the same predicament these days." He closed the chart in front of him. "Even myself. A few years ago, I had the opportunity to move and relocate to Spain with my family. But we decided to stay. Every single day I wonder if I made the right decision."

"Is it possible for Shining Path to defeat our police and military forces and take over the government?"

"And Peru become a communist state?" He shook his head. "I think the chances of that happening are small. But regardless, as long as we have high-level terrorist activity the financial situation of the country will continue to be significantly affected. Our incomes will remain lower compared to physicians in other countries."

"Sometimes I wish the Frenchies would just go and kill them all."

"A lot of people feel that way. But then we wouldn't be much better than the terrorists. The Frenchies are a death squad. Their actions are illegal. We must follow the rule of law, capture the bad guys first, get them in front of a judge and put them in jail for many years."

"I guess you're right," he said looking down. "Why do they call them the Frenchies anyway? "

"One of the very first victims of the terrorists in the eighties was a politician named Franco. Shining Path killed him in front of his wife and children. The first members of this paramilitary group named themselves after him. But Franco means 'French.' It quickly evolved into its nickname of the Frenchies."

"Peruvians love nicknames, right? Anyway, I'm just not feeling very optimistic about the future here. You heard early how much recently graduated doctors are getting paid, right?"

"It's hard to make a living as a general practitioner. Are you thinking of doing a specialty?"

"Yes, preferably one that is procedural-based, like cardiology or gastroenterology, but the problem is the number of spots available is so limited."

"That makes it even more challenging for sure."

"More on a personal level, my Dad thinks that I'm gonna be making a lot of money and I'm gonna be able to finance his retirement."

"It's gonna be a few years before you start bringing decent money home. I think you need to talk to your parents and be clear about their expectations. Also, within the next ten years, chances are you will be married with kids and you will have new responsibilities."

"I'm starting to feel like doing my residency in the United States is gonna be the only option."

"You have to look at all the pros and cons. Many of us just love it here too much. The culture, the food, the music. Our families are here. Emigrating is hard. You leave a lot behind. And you'll be mostly alone for a while. Only you can decide at the end."

Guillermo nodded.

"I'm gonna have to go. It was nice talking to you, Guillermo. Let me know if I can help with anything."

As Casals was leaving the unit, Isabella was walking in, back from the medical school dean's office.

"Hey, how was your meeting with Cazorla?"

"I think it went well. I told him my suspicions, gave him all the information that I had and he's going to talk to the police. He wants to keep everything very confidential because of the hospital's reputation."

"That's good. I hope you are able to stop worrying too much about this issue. It's up to Dr. Cazorla now. By the way, Mario and I are going to Barranco to have beer. Wondering if you wanna join us?" *It would be fun to have her come along.*

"No, thank you. I actually have plans."

"Oh. What are you doing?"

"I'm going to the movies with Freddy."

Freddy! No way. "Alright then. Have a good time."

54

An entire afternoon of meetings and paperwork had left the Archbishop tired and hungry. As he walked the long main hallway of the Archdiocese of Lima towards the kitchen, he could easily recognize the smell of recently baked fresh bread.

"My good friends, what are you doing here?"

"Good evening Monsignor," Father Pedro said with a nervous smile.

Archbishop Villena-Alarcon found the two priests sitting at the table contemplating the two bottles of red wine in front of them.

"We are trying to decide which of these bottles of Rioja we're going to order for the next few months," said Father Manuel.

"Gentlemen," the Archbishop started saying. He knew his delivery could be bombastic at times. "It looks like you are in front of such a delicate enterprise I would dare not to interrupt you. However," he paused for a second and then he added with a big smile, "I hope you don't mind having an extra expert opinion."

"That would be wonderful. Let me get an extra glass for you." Father Pedro could not hide his excitement.

The Archbishop raised the glass of wine against the light and contemplated for a second the beautiful deep red color. He brought the glass close to his nose and smelled the fruity aroma. He took a small sip and let it linger in his mouth as he closed his eyes to distinguish the medium sweetness, the low acidity and the mixed flavors of cherries, plums and a touch of vanilla.

"Lovely! I don't know how you could beat this!"

"We have a winner, then," Manuel said.

"Why don't we get some cheese to go with these, gentlemen? Can you see, Father Pedro, if we have any Manchego?"

"Yes, and maybe some bread and crackers," Pedro added

"Monsignor, you are not gonna watch the night news?" Father Manuel asked.

"I think I'm gonna take a break from the news tonight. I'm actually having a great time with some good old friends right now."

"So are we, Monsignor."

"Did you read about the journalist that was found dead at home?" he said while grabbing a piece of bread.

The two younger priests looked at each other, oblivious. "Not really."

"Brothers, you should watch the news more often. I actually think this regime may be getting rid of some of the people they find to be oppositional to their plans."

"You mean like executing?" Father Manuel asked.

"Yes, but I'm gonna need two more glasses of wine before I can tell you more about it."

"Getting rid of civilians that are not supportive of the government, like a dictatorial regimen?"

"I'm afraid this is just the beginning. It wouldn't surprise me to find myself on the Frenchies' list."

"The Frenchies?"

"That's what they call the most active of the paramilitary groups."

"Please don't say that, Monsignor." Father Pedro looked down.

"Well, just in case," Manuel smiled with complicity. "Let's drink more wine if it happens that this is our last gathering as friends."

"Our Last Supper!" Pedro laughed.

My Last Supper? The words resonated on the Archbishop's head. Then he raised his glass:

"Salud for the Archdiocese of Lima and for all the religious brothers and sisters that work and fight for the poor people of this country!"

55

For being a Friday night, Barranco was not as crowded as usual. Lima's bohemian district with its charming streets, turn-of-the-century buildings and cozy bars and restaurants that draw artists and intellectuals, was a great place to have fun and decompress. It was possible that the most recent terrorist attempts against civilian buildings were making people think twice before going out. Despite that, it was still exciting to be out away from the hospital and the patients.

The waitress was not particularly attractive but had a cute smile and outgoing personality that perfectly matched the establishment. She was also super quick to bring a couple of beers to their table.

"Coming here is like psychiatric prophylaxis," Guillermo said.

"Go to *Delirium* and prevent delirium! That sounds like a great slogan for an advertising campaign," Mario joked while sipping on his beer.

"My social life is so non-existent, it's so pathetic." Guillermo shook his head.

"My friend, you are just a nice guy that wants to find a good girl, get married and live happily forever."

"And you don't?"

"I'm not really in a hurry. I cannot get married until I have enjoyed a plentiful single life, and that won't happen until I'm working as a surgeon and make enough money to have a nice house and a nice car. So at least ten more years."

"That sounds like forever. My most immediate wish is to own a car. I hate taking the bus, and not to mention that without a car dating is so inconvenient."

"Especially when most of the rich girls that you wish you could date live in La Molina far from Miraflores, or Barranco, where all the bars and clubs are."

"Don't date rich girls then?"

"Only regular middle-class girls." Mario laughed while sipping on his beer again. "I've seen the nurse student working in your unit. She is pretty cute. You should ask her out."

"Carmen? Yeah, she seems to be very nice too. I don't think I could date her seriously, though. You know, my Mom will get very upset if I bring home a girlfriend that is a little too dark."

"You couldn't date her because your Mom would think she is a *cholla* from *la sierra*, making her somehow inferior. Sounds like some cast system. Yeah, you mentioned that before. It's sad to hear, especially since I really like your Mom."

"I'm sorry. I know it's horrible."

"Your Mom wants you to marry a rich, white, blonde girl with blue eyes. I don't think those girls go out with broke, uncool medical students. Talking about rich girls, anything going on with your sub-intern Isabella? She is kind of cute."

"She's actually going out on a date with Freddy Revilla."

"Freddy! Really?"

"Looks like a nice guy to me, not a player like his friend Carlos."

"He's a little odd. Maybe because he's an orphan."

"An orphan! Really! I didn't know that."

"His Father died when he was a little boy. Anyway, do you see that girl on the corner?" He pointed to a couple of girls at the opposite side of the pub. "I know her. Her name is Cecilia. Her friend is cute, too. Let's go say hi, talk to them for a while and invite them to my party. We need to recruit more girls."

"Your party! I almost forgot. How are you doing with the preparations?"

"Got pretty much everything we need. We just don't have enough girls, you're gonna have to dance with another guy," he said laughing. "So we better go and say hi to Cecilia and company."

"Let's wait a little bit, okay? I need to loosen up. I need another beer."

"One more beer for my friend!" he told the waitress. "You know, I have never seen you drunk before."

"I only been drunk once in my life."

"Really, only once? No way!"

"Only once, I swear. I went to a new year camping party on the beach. I was so drunk I vomited all over the place. I don't know how I didn't aspirate and die!"

"You lost your chance to die asphyxiated on your vomit like Bon Scott or Jimi Hendrix."

"I guess I lost my chance at immortality. Right?" Guillermo said. He paused for a second thinking. "I cannot let opportunities escape away." He brought the glass up to his lips and took a long swallow. "Okay, let's go and say hi to those girls!"

56

"Two cheeseburgers with fries and two strawberry milkshakes, please" said Freddy to the cashier.

Isabella looked around the place. The new burger joint with its art deco style and neon lights had recently opened and it was one of the trendiest places among young people.

"Sounds delicious," she said with a half-smile. *Probably two-thousand calories.*

"Have you been to this place before?"

"No, I don't really go out a lot, but I heard it's pretty good."

"I think most of us that study medicine become a little socially deprived."

She nodded. Despite the multiple awkward moments of silence since the evening began, Isabella was starting to feel more comfortable next to this boy she just barely met a few days ago.

"How did you like the movie?" he asked as they followed the waiter to their booth.

"It was really good!"

"Clint Eastwood's always been one of my favorite actors but he's also a great director. He made a very special movie, definitely not your typical kind of western."

"Hi guys, two strawberry shakes for you," a female voice interrupted.

"Thank you," he said as the waitress placed two enormous milk-shake glasses on their table.

"Oh my God, this shake is huge!" she said while carefully trying it with a spoon.

Isabella was not wearing her usual dark clothes that she favored while in the hospital; instead she had a white sweatshirt with a multi-color Benetton logo, her favorite GUESS blue jeans and white Reeboks. For a change also, she decided to put a little bit of makeup on.

"You look really nice tonight!"

"Thank you!" she said, feeling the sudden rash of blood in her cheeks. "This shake is so good!"

Isabella had never seen him before wearing anything other than OR scrubs, so it was a little bit of a surprise when he came to pick her up nicely dressed wearing an olive-green long-sleeve shirt and dark blue jeans. His wavy dark brown hair, usually messily falling forward over his forehead, was neatly combed backwards.

"You look nice, too," she said, looking down, trying to avoid eye contact.

"Well, thank you."

The restaurant was overcrowded and loud as expected for a hip new place but despite the noise, they could clearly hear the music playing in the background.

"Cool song," she said as she identified the opening riff of The Cure's "Just Like Heaven."

He nodded. "You like The Cure?"

"Very much."

"Do you have a favorite The Cure song?'

"Not really. They have so many great songs. But the one that comes to my mind right away is "Pictures of You." Not one of the most popular ones, but kind of nostalgic, I guess."

"That's a good song. I have the impression we may like a lot of the same type of music. One of these days you should come over to the house. I have tons of vinyl records and CDs."

"Sounds good."

57

"I'll walk you to the door," Freddy said as he parked his 1980 Datsun Stanza in front of the house.

"You don't need to bother."

"Not a problem," he said as he got out of the car in a hurry and ran to the other side to open her door before she had the chance to do it.

"Thank you." She had always thought that there was nothing more romantic than a man opening the door for a woman.

They walked in silence. Isabella sped up the pace, not knowing what to say and feeling rather uncomfortable.

"I had a great time," he said.

"I had a good time, too. Thank you for the invite."

"I hope we can go out again sometime."

"Yeah, that would be nice."

He looked at her eyes and moved slightly closer. Without saying anything, he put his right hand on her waist, leant forward and gently kissed her lips. An overwhelming spine-tingling chill left Isabella unable to move for an instant and before she even realized, he had already turned around and was walking towards his car.

"Drive safe," she said.

58

When he was first appointed as Bishop of Ayacucho in 1988, Sunday morning service was undoubtedly Father Silvestri's favorite activity. It was the time when he could directly reach the hundreds of members of the parish. And people loved to be close to him, hold his hands and talk about their problems, even for a few minutes, before returning home after mass. Gradually as the terrorist presence of Shining Path continued to grow, his days became so busy that he was already exhausted by the end of the week. Still, the Bishop enjoyed seeing himself delivering the sermon in front of the magnificent cathedral's gold-leaf altar built in the very elaborate Spanish style known as churrigueresque. Getting ready for mass was a small ceremony in itself. As he prepared to dress himself, he first washed his hands.

Give me virtue to my hands, O Lord, that being
Cleansed from all stain I might serve you with
Purity of mind and body.

A knock on the door interrupted his prayer. An altar boy opened the door with extreme caution. "Father Silvestri, sorry to bother you, there is a gentleman here that would like to see you."

He had been waiting for this visit. "Please let him in."

"Father Silvestri, I'm Captain Rincon with military intelligence." Rincon was slender and tall with dark hair and dark copper complexion. He was wearing a blue Members Only jacket and khaki dress pants.

"Captain Milciades Rincon, I get to meet you in person finally. Thank you for coming, please close the door behind you. How was your trip from Lima?" He said as he offered him a chair. "You know we only have a few minutes before mass begins, right?"

"Thank you Father, my visit will be very brief."

"First of all, let me thank you for not wearing your uniform here. I don't wanna give people reasons for all kinds of speculation. I assume your boss is too busy to come and meet with me personally."

"That is correct. The general has his hands full right now, working on multiple strategies to fight the terrorist groups and he thought that I needed to deliver this message as soon as possible."

"I want the general to know that he has one-hundred percent support from the Diocese of Ayacucho and this Bishop."

"The rest of the Catholic Church has not been as welcoming of the government's approach on how to deal with this crisis." Rincon's voice was slow and clear, with a flat tone. The most remarkable thing about him was the complete lack of movement of his face when he spoke.

"Please let your boss know that I met with the Archbishop and offered a pathway for a dignified retirement, but sadly he was not too kind on the idea and strongly declined. I don't think anybody is going to be able to convince the Archbishop to go out without a fight."

"That's very unfortunate."

"It is indeed, but being named after Milciades, the Greek general that defeated the Persians in the battle of Marathon, I have a feeling you already have a plan."

Rincon's expression remained neutral. "I'm delighted to see that Monsignor knows his history very well. We have one of our operatives ready to start working in the Lima Archdiocese to gather as much data as possible."

"Is there anything else I can do to help you today, Captain?"

"The General is requesting that you publicly speak in favor of the death penalty in case of terrorism."

Silvestri suspected that this was coming. He was not unprepared, and the issue had been discussed with Father Andriso before. "That is going to create some problems with most of the other high members of the church."

"We're aware of that, Father. We still don't have any religious personalities that support the government on this issue. We really need your help."

"Tell the general that I will do as he is requesting."

"Excellent. Thank you so much for all your help, Father."

"Where exactly is this agent of yours gonna be working at?"

"At the Archbishop's kitchen."

"Very well, then. Now if you allow me I don't want to be late for Sunday mass."

"I'll see you soon, Bishop Silvestri."

"I hope not. I hope this is the point where you guys take over and you don't need my assistance anymore."

59

By the time it was time to go back to work on Monday morning, Isabella was already mentally exhausted from wondering if everybody in the hospital knew by now that she kissed Freddy Revilla on the first date. He's not even your boyfriend, they'll say. She's such a whore. *But it was not even a real kiss. I actually never kissed him. He got me by surprise. Maybe Freddy didn't tell anybody. He doesn't talk a lot anyway. Whatever.*

"Dr. Casals, I wanted to ask you, where does the nickname "The Cathedral" come from?" Raul the medical student and future radiologist asked as they were finishing rounds.

"It was doctor Carlos Zubieta." Casals couldn't hide a smile remembering his old teacher. "He said if Wembley stadium in London is the cathedral of football, Santa Maria hospital is the cathedral of medicine."

At the same time, I'm fucking twenty-four and this is not fucking high school.

"He was a big football enthusiast. A big time Real Madrid fan. Because my last name, Casals, is actually a Catalan surname, he told me I had to be a Barcelona fan. So that day I was made a Barcelona fan by him."

"How was like rounding with him?" asked Guillermo.

"He was the old-school clinician, who would emphasize the medical history of the patient and the physical exam. I guess he was the closest thing to doing rounds with William Osler." He paused for a second. "Not only that, he would frequently quote Osler's aphorisms."

"Is he still alive?" asked Raul

"Oh, yeah, he's alive and kickin'. He retired several years ago. Used to come often for some of the conferences. One of these days he'll show up for rounds without warning." He stared at the wall for a few seconds. "Okay guys, that's it for today."

As they spread out after rounds Guillermo got closer and whispered to her ear:

"How was your date the other day?"

"It went well."

"Are you gonna go out with him again?"

"I don't know. Maybe."

"I have to place a central line," he said, now with a regular voice. "Mr. Buendia is not tolerating anything by mouth and we're gonna have to start parenteral nutrition. Why don't you help me do it and the next one will be yours?"

"Sounds good."

Guillermo went through all the steps of the procedure with her, as the two of them positioned Mr. Buendia, and placed a long sterile field that covered his entire body.

"Let's clean the area really well. Can you pass me the chlorhexidine please?"

"Here."

"Can you pass me those seven-and-a-half gloves that I left over there? You are gonna look for the triangle formed by the two neck muscles and the clavicle, and are gonna put your lidocaine in the upper corner, right here," he said as he injected the local anesthetic.

"How many have you done?"

"A bunch." He smiled. "Hey I wanted to ask you about your brother, you never finish telling me?"

"Yeah, he moved to the United States to go to college. He wants to major in business."

"That makes him the smart sibling for not choosing medicine. Do you miss him?"

"I miss him a lot." Isabella hesitated for a second. "I haven't really told this to anybody. Sometimes I think the real reason he moved away is because he might be gay. And Peruvian society is not very welcoming of gay people."

"I see." Guillermo didn't look at her, probably feeling uncomfortable. Most Peruvian people would avoid talking about having a closeted gay member in their family.

He advanced the needle until a flow of dark blood came out. "Now that you can see I got good venous return, I'll advance the guide wire."

"But people's lack of acceptance of homosexuality is in part driven by religious ideas and our church is definitely not very sympathetic. That's pretty much when I started reading the Bible looking for answers. Many times, I didn't like what I found."

"What do you mean?"

"You can find a lot of things in the Old Testament that nobody ever mentions in religion class. The Book of Leviticus, for example, says if a man has sexual relations with a man, he should be put to death."

"Then you advance the catheter through the guide wire." He paused for a minute, thinking. "That's in the Old Testament, am I right? I don't think the Catholic Church still thinks that way."

"Yes, it is. But if we believe that the people that wrote the Bible were inspired by God, how can you disregard what is written in the Old Testament?"

"Now you flush your three ports with saline to be sure all of them are working right."

"Looks good."

"Then you suture the skin to secure the line." He then cut the strings with a red scalpel. "And that's it."

"That's a cool scalpel."

"It's a disposable one. It comes with the central line kit."

"Let me see." She retracted the steel blade into the plastic red handle. "Nice. Can I keep it?"

"Sure. It's not sterile anymore."

"That's okay. It's still very sharp. I'll use it as a utility knife." Isabella placed her new toy in her lab coat pocket.

"Now regarding your religion conundrums," he said with a sweet smile. "I'm really sorry. I guess I don't have any answers."

"It's okay. Nobody does. Thank you for the lesson. I'm gonna go outside for a bit. I need to take a break."

Thinking about her brother and religion had put her in a bad mood one more time. She walked outside the unit looking for some breathing space. The day was actually sunny and mildly warm. She stood in front of the nice hospital gardens, closed her eyes and was able to easily perceive the aroma of the flowers in the air. *Such a nice day.*

Out of nowhere, a disheveled male figure appeared in front of her.

"Fuck! You scared me!" It was the morgue guy, the one they called Igor.

"I need to show you something," he said. Without waiting for her to answer, he started walking away.

Does he want me to follow him? "Hey wait! Where are we going?"

"To the morgue!"

Isabella felt her heart pounding in her chest. Was she putting herself at risk, following this creepy guy to his dungeon? As they walked inside the familiar hallway and the very familiar smell, all still fresh in her mind from when she saw Mrs. Jimenez' dead body.

As he reached for the door keys in his dirty white lab coat pocket, she could read his name: "Eduardo Martinez. Lab Tech."

His name is not Igor.

"Remember the patient that you showed me a few weeks ago? The one with the cross on her face?" he asked as he opened the door.

"Of course I remember."

"They brought this patient this morning," he said as he uncovered the corpse lying on the autopsy table. "Does anything get your attention now?"

She looked the body up and down carefully. It was hard not to see. The Egyptian black cross, no more than two centimeters long, was drawn on the patient's left side of the chest. Just like the ones she has seen in the two other cases. There was something very different, though. This patient looked very young.

"How old is he?"

"Twenty-five."

"And how did he die?"

"I have the chart right here. Let me see, it says congestive heart failure."

"But he is too young for that!"

"I'm not the doctor!"

And then all of a sudden, she realized that something was really wrong.

"Shit!" she said.

60

Great group of kids, Casals thought, as he left the medical pavilion and walked towards the doctor's lounge, a small but lovely attending-only getaway. He could have a soda and a sandwich before leaving for his private practice office. He had a very smart and capable team of young doctors that allowed him to elevate the level of the clinical discussions. *Just like when I was an intern rounding with Dr. Zubieta.*

"Dr. Casals?"

He heard somebody calling his name behind him. *Probably one of the students.*

"Hi! Dr. Casals?"

It was not a student. Definitely much older. Mid-fifties maybe. Dark copper skin. He was wearing a white long-sleeve dress shirt and navy-blue dress pants. There was nothing really remarkable about him. A patient's relative, maybe? An old colleague that he could not remember?

"Hi, Dr. Casals. Captain Raymundo Vidal," he said as he showed his police badge and extended his right hand. "Can I ask you a few questions? It shouldn't take too long."

The badge said DINCOTE. Casals recognized the name. The National Counter Terrorism Agency. Casals suddenly felt extremely uneasy. *Why is DINCOTE wanting to talk to me?*

"You don't have to worry, Dr. Casals," said the policeman, probably feeling the physician's apprehension. "I actually happened to be in the hospital visiting one of our colleagues who needed to have surgery, but since I'm here I wanted to ask you a few questions. I'm looking for your medical opinion."

"How do you know about me?"

"I asked the surgery residents who they thought was the best internal medicine doctor and they told me about you and where to find you."

"I see," said Casals, feeling some relief.

Vidal pulled a piece of paper with a list of medications.

"Can you look at these?"

He looked at the list carefully: Hydrocortisone cream, Methyl salicylate gel, Naproxen tablets, Prednisone tablets.

"What kind of patient do you see taking these combinations of medicines?"

"Topical and systemic anti-inflammatories—somebody with joint pain or some type of arthritis could benefit from this. Some inflammatory skin conditions could get better with the topical treatments, too. Prednisone would help in both cases. Naproxen would help joint pain and inflammation."

"Any condition that comes to your mind first?"

"Psoriasis is a chronic inflammatory condition that affects mostly the skin but can cause arthritis too. Also, some connective tissue diseases, like rheumatoid arthritis and lupus."

"Thank you very much Dr. Casals." Vidal interrupted him. "Your help has been invaluable."

"Is that it?"

"You answered my questions very clearly."

"I hope your friend does well."

61

She needed to share her story. She needed to talk to somebody else.

She walked to the surgery ward, but she didn't find the person she was looking for.

She decided to try the residents' rooms building.

Nobody was using the lobby dining table, but she could hear some noise coming from one of the hallways leading to the call rooms. Freddy was standing there in front of one of the lockers.

"Hey there," she said.

"Oh, hi!" Freddy said with a smile.

"What are you doing?"

"I'm updating my stock. Come and take a look. I have an additional locker here where I keep all kinds of stuff that I may need when I'm on call."

Isabella saw inside the locker packed with needles, sterile gloves, catheters, a bottle of normal saline, some meds.

"I even have some amps of epinephrine and atropine for code blues. If there is something that one of your patients cannot have for some reason, let me know. I may be able to help."

"Wow, very nice."

"Thank you."

"Hey listen, I'd like to share something with you, something personal, but not here. At what time are you gonna leave today?"

"I should finish in about an hour."

"Are you gonna be home? Is it okay if I stop by later this afternoon?"

"Of course. That'll be great."

"Okay. See you later."

She walked back to her unit, feeling some relief. She needed to tell Freddy the whole thing. He was very smart and between the two of them they can probably find a way to approach this problem.

"I think I made a mistake, Guillermo," she told her rotation partner.

He put down the chart he was reading. "Why do you say that?"

"The morgue guy just showed me another patient marked with the same Egyptian cross."

"Another case?"

"Yes. But this time, it was a young patient. Not an old, terminal patient, that is suffering or with intractable pain. I read the chart. The final diagnosis was congestive heart failure but it didn't really match the patient's symptoms. That means that the killer is not an angel of mercy and this is more complicated than what I thought."

"Then why would somebody be doing all this?"

"I don't know, but I already talked to Dr. Cazorla and I told him that I suspected Carol. I'm afraid I may get Carol in trouble."

"Oh shit!"

"I may need to go back and talk to him again. But now all my theories have fallen apart. I'm afraid he may dismiss the entire thing."

"I think you should talk to Casals. He'll know what to do."

"You're probably right. But I need a little more time to think about it and come out with an alternative explanation for these deaths. If you have any ideas, please let me know."

62

Archbishop Villena-Alarcon sorely walked down the hallways of Lima's Cathedral staring in silence at the scenes of the Via Crucis on the walls. He stood for a moment in front of a painting of the Virgen de Guadalupe. *My dear lady. You always have shown me the right pathway.* He had not told anybody but he had been seriously considering retiring. *So many things I still have to do.* Leaving his post in a critical moment in the history of the country almost sounds cowardly. Who was going to speak out for the poor? Who was going to call out the government over the lack of justice?

However, he couldn't think of anything more agonizing than saying goodbye to the young boy who had become more than just a secret lover. *My dear Armando, I'm gonna miss you so much.*

He remembered the meeting with Silvestri and his offer, supposedly originating in Rome, was signed by none other than Cardinal Ratzinger.

I should leave on my own terms. But if I don't resign, who knows what Silvestri will do next? More than anything the old Archbishop feared that once gone, Silvestri would likely be the Vatican's choice to become the next leader of the Peruvian Catholic church.

Probably the best was for him to step down, but he needed to be able to pick his successor. There has to be a way. *I need to talk to Esteban. He is the only one I can trust.*

He walked to his office in a hurry and picked up the phone.

"Dear Esteban, I think it's time for me to step down from my position as Archbishop."

63

"Is your Mom home?"

"No, she had to go to my Grandma's. She should be back soon," Freddy said, holding the door open for her.

As Isabella walked in, she examined the simple Spanish-style house with white walls and dark brown hardwood floors. "You have a very nice house."

"Thank you."

The thought of being home alone with a guy she just started dating surprisingly did not make her feel uncomfortable as she would have anticipated. Actually, all the opposite. She felt safe.

"Your Mom is very pretty," she said, looking at a portrait on the hallway table. "I can't wait to meet her."

"We don't get along very well."

Isabella wanted to tell him that she was sorry, but she wasn't sure that was the most appropriate thing to say. She knew at some point they were going to talk about more personal things and she could share how she didn't get along with her Dad, either.

"My bedroom is this way."

The hallway led to a larger-than-average-size bedroom with a twin bed against the wall and a desk at the opposite side. Posters of rock bands on the walls, shelves with books. But more than anything, lots of vinyl records, cassettes and CDs.

"It looks like you spend all your money on music."

"Yeah, pretty much."

"How many records do you have here?"

"I haven't counted in a while. More than fifty for sure," he said casually.

She noted the record player.

"Can I play something?"

"Of course."

She saw The Beatles' "Revolver" black-and-white record jacket on his desk.

"Most of the Beatles music I heard is from their earlier albums. I haven't listened to a lot of their later stuff. Why is 'Revolver' such an important record?"

"At that time the Beatles had full creative control of their music. So, they wanted to experiment and create something very different. They used a lot of new recording technology, Indian and classical instruments not commonly used in pop music, and the songs all have different styles. For a lot of people, 'Revolver' is the Beatles best album."

She loved listening to him talking about music. So confident and knowledgeable. His voice sounded like he could be directing a radio show.

"That's very interesting. Can I play it?"

"Go ahead, please."

"I remember when I was little, my Mom used to play "Hard Day's Night" almost every day."

"Can I bring you something to drink? A lemonade maybe?"

"Lemonade would be great, thank you."

"Ok. I'll be back right away."

Isabella looked around the room one more time. *What kind of books do you have?*

She laughed to herself at the idea of trying to figure out a person based on his tastes for books and music, but she was getting more intrigued by this guy and so far, she liked what she was seeing.

She recognized some of the titles right away: *Guyton's Physiology, Netter's Anatomy of the Nervous System, Harrison's Principles of Internal Medicine,* but also she was happy to see Vargas Llosa's *La Guerra del Fin del Mundo,* Gabriel Garcia Marquez' *Cien Años de Soledad* and many history books.

Then she looked at a bunch of disorganized papers on the desk. Medical school stuff, syllabus, schedules. Under all that, she found a black cover notebook.

She flipped through the pages and found what looked like poems or maybe song lyrics that she didn't recognize. *Does he write songs, too?* Unfinished drawings of what appear to be a church, symbols that were unknown to her and… a cross.

Suddenly Isabella felt her heart racing. It couldn't be possible. She looked again. There was no doubt. It was an Egyptian cross. Just like the ones she had seen on the victims.

She got up and quickly felt her heart pounding against her chest, her vision turning blurry and her hands shaking uncontrollably. She had never felt so scared before.

She put the notebook down when she saw Freddy standing by the door with a glass of lemonade.

"Are you okay? You look kind of pale."

"I don't feel good. I'm sorry. I need to go home right now."

64

"You know, dear Armando..." Archbishop Villena-Alarcon's post-dinner reflections were usually not optimistic. "Lima was actually a very lovely city back in the 1950s."

"That's what I heard, Father."

"I had to go to Villa El Salvador this morning. Have you been there? Huge town! Anyway, we drove around for over an hour to get there, and you know what? I didn't even recognize this place anymore. Lima, the City of Kings! The Pearl of the Pacific! What happened to Lima?" He paused, his eyes full of grief. "What happened to our city? Terrible traffic, overcrowded streets and so much poverty! It's so depressing. And on top of everything there's so much violence and so many innocent people dying. It makes me very sad, Armando."

"I'm sorry you feel that way, Father. Would you want me to turn the TV on?"

"Yes, please. Earlier this year Shining Path murdered a young community organizer in Villa El Salvador in front of her children. You must have heard about it."

"Yes, Father."

"I got to meet and talk to some of her friends and the people that knew her. It was a very touching moment." The Archbishop paced around the room. His voice, normally deep and powerful, sounded tired instead.

"You know, I have dedicated all my energy to speak against this ongoing war. I've been invited to TV, given interviews to newspapers and magazines and written a couple of opinion articles for *El Comercio*. The Catholic Church cannot stay silent. We did not denounce fascism in Mussolini's Italy or Franco's Spain, and probably didn't do enough to prevent Hitler from murdering Jews. We must denounce when the government's military response is leading to more atrocities; otherwise history will not forgive us. We cannot stay silent or become pro-militaristic like Silvestri is doing. We must denounce."

The older priest sat down slowly. His feet hurt. He felt exhausted. For how much longer was he going to be able to do this job?

At the moment the TV news program showed a short version of an interview Bishop Juan Carlos Silvestri had just given to Channel 3 from Spain.

"Monsignor, would you like me to bring you some of your favorite wine?" asked the young seminarian.

The Archbishop raised his index finger without taking his eyes from the TV set.

To the reporter's question regarding the controversial issue of the death penalty for terrorist cases, Silvestri responded: "We cannot be cowards. We are living in a time where firmness and manhood are needed. Our country needs to support the death penalty."

Villena-Alarcon looked down, feeling defeated.

"Yes. That would be lovely, my dear friend." *No. I can't step down right now. This country needs me more than ever.*

Then he looked up at Armando with a determined smile. "Please bring me some of the Rioja that I like so much and come sit next to me. I could use some company right now."

65

Isabella left Freddy's house as fast as she could despite his repeated protests. Her heart was still beating out of control. As she rushed to her truck, she heard a loud voice behind her. "Stop right there!"

It wasn't Freddy. She turned around and saw a male figure wearing olive-green military clothes.

"Isabella Castle, you need to come with us."

"What?" At that moment everything felt extremely confusing. "Sorry, but you're mistaken, sir," she said, annoyed, looking in a different direction, trying to hide the tears in her eyes.

"Please come with us and do not resist!"

"Sorry, I think you got the wrong person. Why would you want me to come with you?"

"You're being detained for suspicion of terrorist activity."

She started to say "That doesn't make any sense" when she felt the full power of the man's fist against the middle of her abdomen that caused her upper body to fall forward and brought her down to her knees. Trying to catch her breath, she saw a second man coming.

Between the two, they carried her into a black SUV, as she kicked and screamed hopelessly. Everything happened extremely fast. It felt almost like a blurry dream except her belly hurt like it was going to explode any time.

Once in the back seat of the car, the soldier next to her put a canvas bag over her head.

"Stay quiet or I'll have to punch you again!"

66

Bishop Juan Carlos Silvestri couldn't sleep. He had unsuccessfully tried for hours, before realizing that it was better to stop fighting. He got out of bed, put on a heavy winter coat and walked to the little patio next to his bedroom. It was cold outside but it didn't matter, he had always enjoyed being able to look up and see the innumerable tiny stars scattered over the clear mountain sky of Ayacucho's nights. Captain Rincon had called him earlier that evening and delivered some terrible news. He lit a cigarette and took a slow deep breath and his vision quickly became fuzzy as the tears started to build up. *Forgive me, Lord. It didn't have to be this way. But that old obstinate bastard would not quit.*

67

Monsignor Villena-Alarcon looked at the clock. It was now past midnight and he had suddenly woken up not feeling well. Armando had already left a while ago. He could not get comfortable. Some discomfort in the chest. *It's probably just heartburn. I need to get some TUMS.* It's probably the wine. Maybe that Rioja the brothers chose wasn't as good. He reached to the bedside table lamp and turned the lights on. Got up slowly and walked towards the bathroom but after a few steps everything in front of him started to get foggy. He saw the room in front of him moving up and down, as if he was on a boat in the middle of the ocean. Then he felt his lower body becoming weak.

"Help! Help!" He tried to say, but the words could barely come out before the lights went off and he fell down to the floor.

68

By the time Jorge Casals arrived at the hospital the next morning, it was obvious that something unusual was happening. He soon learned. Archbishop Villena-Alarcon, the head of the Catholic Church in Peru had been found unresponsive on his bedroom floor. He was taken to Santa Maria Hospital just a few miles from his residency. Shortly upon arrival, the emergency physicians decided to place a breathing tube and put him on mechanical ventilation as he was not able to protect his airway. His blood pressure was low. Two large-bore intravenous lines were placed on each arm and fluid resuscitation was started. His initial lab results were consistent with acute renal failure. He was then admitted to the Intensive Care Unit, where a team of critical care medicine specialists took over his care.

The morning news reporters emphasized that the president himself had called the Minister of Health, Dr. La Mota, to be sure the priest received the best possible care.

The presence of the very important patient was very well noticed by all the hospital staff. TV channels and groups of journalists camped around Santa Maria's gardens. Heavy security from police and secret service was also present. Politicians and congressmen looking for some attention made quick stops to express their sympathies in front of the cameras, as the ICU visits remained strictly restricted.

"Do you know what happened to the Archbishop, Dr. Casals?" asked Guillermo just before getting started with morning rounds.

"Not much other than what they say on TV. He was found minimally responsive on the ground at home. His blood pressure was low. He was intubated for airway protection. He's on a ventilator now. If I had to guess, I would say he has overwhelming sepsis. A common condition for the elderly. He was also taken for a CT of the head to rule out an acute stroke. That's as much as I know. They're only allowing the ICU team to have access to the chart and the lab results."

Guillermo and Raul looked discouraged. Casals felt sorry for them. These young men were going through a lot: terrorism, social and financial instability, and now this. The Archbishop was a very popular figure. He was not only the representative of God himself but also a bastion of social justice. A defender of the poor. It wasn't fair. He knew life wasn't fair either, but he wished he could do something.

"Guys, if you are not busy now, why don't we go to the attending lounge and have something to drink." The young doctors appeared a little confused.

"I've never been to the attending lounge before. Are we even allowed there?" Raul asked.

"Don't worry about it. You're coming with me," Casals said with a smile. "By the way, where is Isabella? Is she supposed to be off today?"

"I haven't heard from her, sir. She must be sick. I'll call her at home later," Guillermo said.

The attending lounge was small but welcoming with a couple of leather chairs and a big-screen TV. It had its own kitchen where food was prepared for the members of the medical staff.

A framed poster of Santa Maria Hospital on the wall greeted the visitors.

Casals looked at it and shook his head in disapproval.

"Is there something wrong with the poster, sir ?" Guillermo asked. "It's brand new, isn't it? I think it looks very nice."

Casals shrugged his shoulders but did not say anything.

"I like, for example, that they made the letters in purple, a color always associated with wisdom and royalty," Guillermo added.

"It's not that. I do like the purple too. I'm getting a coffee. What do you guys want to drink?"

"Inka Kola, please. What is it, then?" Guillermo insisted.

"It's the Caduceus," replied Casals. "I advised them not to use it for their design."

"I'll have an Inka Kola diet, please. The Ca... What did you just say sir?" Raul asked.

"The Caduceus," Guillermo said. "Caduceus is the staff of the Greek god Hermes. Or Mercury for the Romans."

"Exactly. There is this misconception that the Caduceus, the winged staff entwined by two serpents, is the symbol of medicine." He couldn't avoid sounding irritated.

Raul looked at the hospital poster again. He could see the two snakes. "Is it not?"

"No! The symbol of medicine is actually the rod of Asclepius. One single snake. No wings," said Casals.

"I'm sorry, doctor Casals, I don't know a lot about history or who Asclepius was." Raul had no problems showing his lack of knowledge.

"Asclepius is the Greek god of medicine."

"One wing or two wings, does it really make a difference?"

"A lot of people identify the Caduceus as the symbol of medicine, especially after it was mistakenly used by the U.S. Army in the early nineteen-hundreds. The problem that I have is, and I take this personally, the Caduceus is associated with Hermes, god among other things of commerce, trading and thieves. I don't think that's how medicine wants to be defined. The rod of Asclepius, on the other hand, brings you back to the ancient and more pure origins of the art of healing."

69

Bishop Silvestri had just grabbed a copy of Saint Augustine's *The City of God* from the bookcase when he heard the approaching noises of a person running down the long hallway of the diocese of Ayacucho.

"Father Silvestri, may I come in?" A young priest gently opened the library door. "I'm really sorry to bother you, but you have a phone call," he said with a timid voice. "The person on the line says it's a very urgent matter."

The Bishop gave the young man a contemptuous glance and quickly returned to his office resigned not to have some quiet time for himself.

"Father Silvestri speaking."

"Good morning, Father, this is Captain Rincon. By now you've probably already seen the news about Archbishop Villena- Alarcon."

"I'm sorry captain, but I haven't watched TV today. What happened?"

Silvestri knew that talking on the phone with a military operative was potentially dangerous. It was possible that The Doc was listening or even recording this conversation.

"The Archbishop is sick, in critical condition. He's been admitted to the intensive care unit of Santa Maria Hospital."

"What happened to him? Is he awake?" He tried to appear concerned and made an effort to keep the number of words to a minimum and to not say anything incriminating.

"I have one of my guys following the case closely. There is going to be a news conference later today. So far, the official medical report is that he has a severe gastrointestinal infection leading to dehydration and low blood pressure. The truth is he's in shock, his organs are failing and he's been kept sedated on mechanical ventilation."

Silvestri shook his head in disbelief. So many times, it felt like he was surrounded by a bunch of incompetent people.

"Is he gonna be okay? Do we know?"

"The doctors are somewhat optimistic and feel his chances of surviving this illness are higher than fifty percent."

Those are pretty good chances. "Pretty good chances I'd say. I will pray for him, Captain. Thank you for letting me know."

"Don't hang up yet, Father. There is one more thing," said Rincon, making a pause for a few seconds. "The general would like to meet with you in person as soon as possible. I'm sending a military plane that will pick you up from the air force base in about three hours."

Fuck. "Very well, Captain."

He walked outside slowly. I'm gonna meet with The Doc, he thought. Something that he had been trying to avoid. He lit a cigarette nervously, and then another one and another; still, he was not able to stop his lower lip from shaking.

70

The doctor's lounge TV did not stop showing updates about the health of the Archbishop. A veteran broadcaster had just announced an unconfirmed report that the Archdiocese of Lima was requesting for the prelate to be transferred to Clinica Internacional, a prestigious private hospital in the city.

"If the Archbishop was to die, who do you think would benefit the most?" Guillermo asked without turning his attention away from the TV set.

"What a weird question! " Raul said. "Does everything that happens have to be some sort of conspiracy?"

"If that happens, I'm sure the President will not shed a tear," Casals said.

"How is that?" Raul asked.

"Villena-Alarcon has been very critical of the government, from the economic policies that mostly benefit big corporations to the military response to Shining Path." He thought for a few seconds and then he continued. "And also…" only to stop himself again in the middle of the sentence.

"What?" Guillermo was now fully invested in the conversation.

"Well, Opus Dei."

"Opus Dei? The Catholic order? Why?" Raul asked

"Opus Dei is not really an order like the Jesuits or the Franciscans. They do have a unique organization within the Catholic Church, but in any case, the group has gained a lot of power during this government term. Father Silvestri, the Bishop of Ayacucho, is a member of the Opus Dei. Even the minister of health is an Opus Dei supernumerary."

"Supernumerary? What is that?"

"I know." Guillermo tried to help. "A lay person, usually a married man with a family, most commonly a professional like a lawyer or a doctor that devotes time and money to the organization."

"That is correct," Casals said. "If the Archbishop dies, Silvestri will probably become the most visible candidate to become the leader of the Catholic Church in Peru, the new Archbishop and with time potentially a Cardinal."

"Does being a Cardinal come with some special implications?" Guillermo asked.

"When a Pope dies, cardinals from all over the world are called to be part of the conclave to elect the new Pope among themselves."

"Fuck!" Raul yelled "Silvestri is gonna be the next Pope!"

71

Isabella woke up on the floor of an eight-by-eight-foot dark room with no windows. A single light bulb hanging from the middle of the ceiling provided minimal illumination. Somewhere along the way she had passed out. She couldn't see where she was taken but the ride did not take more than an hour and therefore she was still in Lima. The last thing she remembered was screaming, asking for answers. She sat down on the ground, took her shoes off and massaged her feet for a few minutes. Her belly still hurt badly from the soldier's punch. She looked around her cell. The room had unfinished brick walls and concrete floors and it felt cold and moist.

A young man in military clothes opened the door and brought a glass of milk and a piece of bread. "You should eat some."

But she couldn't. Although she had not eaten in hours, the combination of fear and pain was too much to overcome. By now her parents were probably worried that she had not come home yet and had likely called the police reporting her missing. Multiple images invaded her mind chaotically. She had heard multiple stories of people taken away by the military that were never seen again. Stories of women that were raped before they were executed. Who were her captors? Did somebody make a mistake accusing her of being a terrorist? Or was somebody mad that she was investigating the murders at the hospital? And if that was the case, was it Cazorla who pointed at her? Is he associated with one of the government's paramilitary groups? Has she been taken by the infamous Frenchies? And Freddy, how does he fit in all of this? Was he actually the Cathedral serial killer? So many unanswered questions.

72

Back on the medical ward, as he speeded up to catch up with the work, Guillermo wondered if the day was going to get any weirder. Then he saw Andrea coming his way.

"Hey Guillermo, have you seen Isabella today?" she asked.

"No, she didn't come to work today. I was wondering if she's at home sick."

"No. Her Mom called me. She didn't come home last night. She's never done anything like this before. I'm really worried about her."

"Shit!" He thought for a second. "She went out with Freddy the other day. Why don't we go look for him and see if he knows anything?"

As they walked towards the surgery building Guillermo couldn't stop himself from asking: "Does she like Freddy?"

"I think she does. They have a few things in common. To begin with, they are both socially inept individuals," she said with a half-smile.

"He seems a bit off, don't you think?"

"Well, I know he had a tough childhood, his Dad died when he was a toddler."

"Do you know how he died?"

"It's actually a very sad story. Freddy's Dad was a young doctor, married with a little child. Anybody would call it a perfect home."

"And what happened?"

"He committed suicide."

"Oh shit! That's horrible! Why?"

"Nobody really knows. Dr. Alejandro Cazorla, the Dean, was actually a good friend of his Father. Same medical school class. He stepped up to support Freddy's Mom. So he became like a second Father or a Father figure, if you want."

"Wow, good for Dr. Cazorla, it looks like he's always been a nice guy."

"So, yeah, he is a little odd but there was a lot of tragedy in his life and he seems to be handling things very well now."

"Well, let's go see if he has any idea where she is at."

73

Silvestri's plane landed on time at an air force base right outside Lima. A vehicle was waiting to take him to a San Isidro Hotel where he had already been checked in under a fake name. A military operative wearing civilian clothes was assigned to him, and remained outside his hotel suite at all times. Nobody from his diocese knew that he had traveled to the capital. He was told to remain in his room and to wait for further instructions. That evening he was going to meet face to face with Valentin Montero, better known as The Doc. He knew that this meeting could have a major impact on the future of the Catholic Church in Peru. He kneeled down and rested his elbows on the bed and closed his eyes. *Help me, Lord. Give me the strength I need to protect your church.*

As he prepared for the encounter, he opened his suitcase and removed a long-sleeve black shirt that he ironed as he continued to pray...*and lead us not into temptation, but deliver us from evil.* He opened a pocket of his toiletry bag where his Seiko chronograph was. La Mota had told him that The Doc was a watch enthusiast with a large collection of expensive timepieces. He wondered what he would be wearing that evening. A *Patek Phillipe?*

Father Silvestri himself wore an inexpensive Casio most days, but you don't happen to meet the most powerful man in Peru every day. This was a special occasion. The Seiko had a unique look with its yellow dial and its blue and red "Pepsi" bezel. The Bishop had learned its history from a watch connoisseur, a Swiss ambassador he met in Rome many years ago. After being worn by Colonel William Pogue on a NASA mission to space, it had been renamed *The Pogue* by horology aficionados. It was not an expensive watch by any means, which it wouldn't be appropriate for a priest to wear in a country where so many children go to bed hungry. But at the same time his Seiko had a rich history that any serious watch enthusiast would recognize.

Even Pope John Paul II wore a two-tone Rolex Datejust. So, one day, he thought, after becoming a Cardinal, it would be the right time to get what he called his grail watch: an understated black-dial Rolex Explorer. *Someday when I'm back in Rome.*

74

As soon as Guillermo and Andrea walked into the surgery ward, they were quickly welcomed by the putrid stench of an infected wound.

"Hey Carlos!" Andrea said, while covering her nose and mouth with her right hand.

Carlos, who had just removed the surgical dressings of a patient's abdomen, looked very happy to see them. "Hey hi guys! Nice to see you, Andrea, and welcome to the awesome world of surgery!" He didn't seem bothered by the strong smell.

"We were looking for Freddy. Is he around?" she asked.

"Freddy, Freddy," he said, shaking his head. "He came this morning like every day but then he said he had to leave early, that he had something urgent to do. I don't know what or where, but now I have to finish his work too!" He looked annoyed.

"Did he say anything else?" Guillermo asked

"Sorry, he didn't."

"We're looking for Isabella. She didn't come to work. Did you know Freddy and her went on a date a couple of nights ago?" Andrea asked.

"Ah!" he said, surprised. "No, he didn't tell me. But good for him!"

Then he turned towards Guillermo. "Don't forget we have a party!"

Mario's party! I almost forgot!

Andrea glared at Carlos like she wanted to punch him.

"Would you be going, Andrea? It should be fun!"

75

Bishop Silvestri arrived at the upscale San Isidro penthouse ten minutes late. There were multiple black SUVs parked around the building and multiple security men along the way to the front door. Silvestri was wearing a dark gray Trilby hat, black suit and a black shirt. He decided not to wear his clerical collar like he always did. He recognized most of the people inside. He sat down in the only empty chair available and pulled a pack of cigarettes from inside his jacket. The condo was decorated with exquisite good taste. The furniture looked expensive but not gaudy, and hanging from the wall were a few modern art pieces. Most likely the work of a professional interior designer, the Bishop thought.

"Nice place you have here, Augusto. You don't mind if I smoke, do you?" he said while lighting a cigarette.

Dr. Augusto La Mota , ex director of Santa Maria Hospital and the current Minister of Health, was the host, and as such he occupied the Churchill-style brown leather chair in the center of the living room. Dr. Alejandro Cazorla, Dean of the medical school, was sitting next to him.

"Father, let me introduce you to Dr. Alejandro Cazorla."

"Very nice to meet you, Father Silvestri," he said.

The Dean looked patently nervous.

The other person in the room was the one they all called The Doc. He didn't need to be introduced. He remained sitting calmly on his chair with a neutral expression. His dark hair was slicked back, making his aquiline nose look even bigger. His big golden-frame glasses matched his watch. Silvestri noted he was wearing a gold Rolex Day Date, the so-called "President's watch." The watch had acquired such a nickname after American president Lyndon Johnson wore it while in office. For Silvestri this was an obvious statement of authority. Wearing that watch meant he was the person in power. The real president was sitting in front of him right now, staring at the wall with a slight grin. *Excellent choice for a watch, Doc. You didn't disappoint me.*

Silvestri's attention suddenly focused on one of the paintings. He got up and walked towards the abstract artwork on the wall. "Is this an original Fernardo de Szyszlo's piece?"

La Mota nodded proudly. "Yes, it is indeed, Father."

"Very nice, Augusto, but I'm still not sure why I was asked to come tonight," Cazorla said, looking inpatient. Then he turned towards The Doc. "Before we start I have a question for you, General. I have been told Raymundo Vidal from DINCOTE has been seen in the hospital asking questions to some of our doctors and staff. Does this meeting have anything to do with him?"

"Raymundo Vidal!" He laughed. "The poor Raymundo with his little intelligence unit doesn't know what the hell he's doing. Their methods are totally outdated. They got nothing. Please don't worry about him. He doesn't know anything about this meeting." He paused for a few seconds and then spoke with a more serious demeanor.

"Gentleman, good evening and thank you for being here. In order to begin, I would like Bishop Silvestri to give us a little introduction about the situation we're dealing with."

Silvestri knew the reason he was needed there.

"Good evening, gentlemen. First of all, I would like to thank General Montero, for making this meeting possible. Our society has been going through incredible changes since the sixties and seventies. The demographic explosion around our capital cities, especially Lima, and the immense levels of poverty millions of Peruvians live with day after day. Socialist theories have failed, despite the academic sociologists trying to brainwash us all of the opposite. These socialist ideas have their religious version in the theology of liberation that has dominated some of the thinking among the Catholic Church leaders in Latin America. My beloved country is now in the middle of a war against an extremist group that we need to win at all costs. Our response has to be unforgiving. We need to strongly support our government and our military. We cannot win this war if our church keeps reminding us that we need to worry about the human rights of the fucking terrorists. The Catholic Church plays a major role in Peruvian society. In order to defeat terrorism, our government, military and church need to work together. We need to be an alliance. I think we all here can agree on that. Gentlemen, our country needs a new group of leaders in our church."

"Yes, of course we do, your excellence," said The Doc, nodding his head. "Doctor Cazorla and Doctor La Mota, we desperately need your help in this matter." He paused and looked directly into their eyes. "You can help all the citizens of this country."

Silvestri then opened his Bible. "I would like to read a passage from 1 Samuel 15:

"This is what the Lord Almighty says: I will punish the Amale-kites for what they did to Israel when they waylaid them as they came up from Egypt. Now go attack the Amalekites and totally destroy all that belongs to them. Do not spare them: put to death men and women, children and infants, cattle and sheep, camels and donkeys."

He then closed the book and looked at the men in front of him. "Gentleman, sometimes when you fight against the evil enemies of the Lord you have to be merciless."

"Thank you, Father," said The Doc. "Gentleman, yesterday, Arch-bishop Villena -Alarcon was admitted to the hospital severely ill."

"We are aware of that," Cazorla said. "He's in the intensive care unit. On mechanical ventilation."

The Doc slowly turned his eyes towards him, obviously bothered, probably not used to being interrupted. "That's correct. This meeting was called urgently as the Archbishop may be moved to Clinica Inter-nacional. Once he is there, we may not have another opportunity to get things done."

"I have a question for Father Silvestri," Cazorla said, looking at the Doc. "Let me ask you, Father, isn't the Archbishop your boss?"

"Not really. No. Pope John Paul II named the Opus Dei as his personal prelature. That means Opus Dei is governed from Rome directly instead of the local diocese. The Archbishop is not my boss. But I do have a lot of respect for him. Archbishop Villena-Alarcon has served our Lord with his best intentions. He was given the opportu-nity to step aside from his position and unfortunately he has declined."

"Father Silvestri," The Doc said, "Thank you very much for coming to our meeting. I will manage from here. A plane is waiting for you to take you back to Ayacucho tonight."

"Thank you for having me. Have a good night, gentlemen," Silvestri said. As he got up, he heard Cazorla asking, "What are we gonna do with the girl?"

The priest turned around. "The girl? What girl are we talking about?"

"Isabella Castle, she's one of our students," said Cazorla.

"Gentlemen. You don't have to worry about it. I'll take care of that," the Doc said, clearly irritated. "Now let's go back to our business."

As the driver opened the door and he entered the car, Silvestri wondered if The Doc had noticed his Seiko Pogue.

76

Isabella's cell did not receive any natural light so she couldn't tell what time it was. How many hours have gone by? For how long has she lay motionless on the floor? She wished she had a wristwatch. *If I get out of here alive, I'll get one. Maybe a Swatch on some crazy colors.*

If I get out of here alive? She was starting to lose any hope. She wondered if her captors, probably men from a paramilitary group, were debating which way to kill her and how to dispose of her body, or were maybe waiting for orders from their leader.

It was getting more and more chilly. The rough concrete floor felt cold beneath her feet and she put her shoes back on. Then she suddenly felt the need to urinate.

"Excuse me!" she yelled. "I need to go to the bathroom!"

But nobody answered.

She was eating a piece of bread from earlier that was already hard to bite, when the door opened.

"Did you say you need to go to the bathroom?" the man said.

"Yes, please."

"Fuck!" he said, rolling his eyes. "Wait a second," and he closed the door.

About five minutes later, he was back.

"This way," the man said.

She followed him through a long hallway. He could see him better now. He looked very young, probably early twenties. He had dark hair and dark eyes and avoided looking straight at her eyes. He was wearing a camouflage military uniform and was carrying a short barrel rifle.

"There, at the end of the hall to the right. I'll be waiting for you. You have five minutes."

"Thank you."

Isabella washed her face and hands, and stood there for a few seconds looking around for any ways to escape, but there were not any windows there either. She closed her eyes and leaned back against the door when she heard the guard talking to somebody else. She could only hear short pieces of the conversation.

"I won't be able to go with you guys...something came up... Santa Maria Hospital...big fucking deal tonight..."

Did he just say Santa Maria Hospital?

77

Guillermo was very aware his team did not look fully engaged during rounds. Despite Casals doing his best effort to make this teaching session as good as possible, they were all worried about Isabella still missing.

Raul presented the last case of the morning, a young boy with new-onset seizures caused by a parasitic condition of the brain called cysticercosis.

"Actually, cysticercosis is the most common cause of epilepsy in many countries in the developing world," said Casals. "In ancient times , it was thought that epilepsy was caused by the Gods . The Greeks called it the sacred disease. However, Hippocrates wrote that men thought epilepsy was divine because they did not understand it. One day, he said, we will understand what causes epilepsy and we will cease to believe it's divine. And so, it is with everything in the universe."

Guillermo understood the hidden meaning behind Hippocrates' teaching, but Hugo and Raul looked confused. "Between you and Isabella, I may become agnostic by the end of the rotation."

"No news from her yet?" Casals asked.

"No, sir. She's still missing."

"She's a very smart girl. She is gonna be okay"

"Can I talk to you for a second?" Guillermo asked after they finished their rounds.

"Yes. Something I should know?" Casals asked.

"I'm worried about Isabella, sir. For the last several weeks, she's been obsessed with thinking there is an angel of mercy serial killer in the hospital murdering old terminally ill patients. The perpetrator leaves a signature mark on their bodies: a black cross."

Casals raised his eyebrows and opened his mouth like he was ready to say something. But he didn't.

"The day before she disappeared she went to see Dean Cazorla to tell him about her theory. But then she found a younger patient with the same sign of the cross mark that didn't match the victims' profile."

Casals looked down and shook his head. "I need to go!" he said abruptly.

"Dr. Casals, something wrong?"

But he didn't answer.

78

Captain Raymundo Vidal had just returned to his office from a late dinner at Cordano, the historic old restaurant in downtown Lima, and was hoping to call it a day and go home soon when an urgent phone call interrupted his post-meal reflections. He got up from his desk and called his two most trusted DINCOTE officers.

He gave one of them a piece of paper with a name on it. "I want you to get on the phone right now and call all your military contacts and find out where they're keeping this person, and I want you to call me on the radio as soon as you know anything. Understood?"

"Yes sir. But what about our Guzman operation? I think we are getting very close."

"It's on hold for now. We've got another priority to deal with."

Then he looked at the second one "You are coming with me. We're gonna visit a couple of our army friends that owe us some favors."

"Sir, is this mission related to terrorist activity?"

"Not necessarily," Vidal said. "But sometimes you have to do the right thing. Especially when God himself is calling you for help."

The officer gave him a puzzled look. "Excuse me, captain, did you say God?"

79

Cazorla was not in his office. The secretary said he had arrived at the school administration building on time as usual but after a couple of early meetings he had left. She also mentioned he looked distracted and not engaging like his normal self.

Casals first looked for him at the main library where the two of them used to navigate among the medical journals, sometimes trying to find an answer to a clinical question but sometimes just for fun. Casals missed those days. Engaged in the art of medicine without attachments or worries. The purest form of love. But his old classmate wasn't there. He then quickly stopped by the anatomy amphitheater, the biochemistry lab and the main auditorium. But Cazorla wasn't there either.

He finally walked down the halls of the old building where the dean's office and the administration used to be when the school first opened in the 1950's.

Cazorla was there, staring at the picture of the 1978 class.

"Hi, Alejandro."

He turned his head almost in slow motion. He looked like he had aged twenty years all of a sudden. His hair, which was light brown and blondish, had turned salt-and-pepper gray. A day or two of unshaved coarse beard covered his jaw and cheeks.

"Where is Isabella?" Casals asked.

"I don't know," he said. His eyes were bloodshot and weary and the circles below his eyes had never seemed more prominent, like he had not slept for days.

"What happened? You look like shit."

"They have her."

"Who are they?"

Cazorla shook his head and turned towards the picture on the wall.

"Remember those days? Things were so good those days."

"Those were great days and we can still have many more great days to come."

Cazorla shook his head again and looked down.

"Alejandro, what have you done? Where is Isabella?"

"I didn't want to do it, Jorge, but he made me."

"He? Who is he?"

He looked at Casals, his eyes widened in fear. "The Doc, Jorge, The Doc!"

80

"Something wrong, Guillermo? It seems like you are not paying attention to what I'm saying," Mario said.

"I'm sorry, I'm really distracted." Guillermo closed the patient record he was working on. "Something is going on here. First Isabella disappears and then my attending leaves us. I think Casals may know something. I really hope Isabella is not in trouble."

"You're overreacting. It's gonna be okay. It's probably something really mundane. I'm sure she's fine, seriously! I just wanted to be sure you're still coming to my party."

"I don't know, man, I don't feel good about this whole thing."

"Brother, I had driven all the way from my hospital just to be sure that one of my best friends is coming to my party. Let me tell you. I know Isabella is fine. She is okay. I know that for a fact. You know what? She may even show up to the party at the last minute."

Guillermo looked down and rubbed the side of his neck.

"Remember Stella, the girl we met the other night in Barranco? Well, I know for a fact she is coming."

"Stella is coming?"

"Yes, she meets all the criteria you're looking for in a girl and I'm sure your Mom will approve. And, one more thing, Cecilia told me that she asked about you."

"Did she?" Something to look forward to, he thought. "I guess there is no way I'm not coming then."

81

Isabella had fallen asleep again when her cell door opened.

"It's time to go," the guard said.

She got up with some difficulty. Her body was sore and her joints were stiff. How many hours had she been here in this state of semi-consciousness? Now awake all of a sudden, she couldn't stop thinking her time was up. Few years ago, when she battled with depression, Isabella had thought about suicide. Maybe she had no care about her life so much back then. But now she wanted to live. She desperately needed to. God plays with our mortal lives in mysterious and wicked ways. They were coming for her now. The worst imaginable thing is finally going to happen. She won't have the chance to say goodbye to her parents. She won't ever get to see her brother Diego again. And she won't be able to stop Freddy from killing patients at The Cathedral. She walked outside her cell slowly. Next to the guard on military clothes there was a middle-aged man with black hair and copper skin who was wearing dress clothes. He must be one of the bosses, she thought.

"Please, sir, I swear I'm innocent," she started begging. What else could she do?

"Hi, Miss Castle. I'm Captain Raymundo Vidal. I'm taking you home."

She didn't know what to say. The man was probably lying for her to stop talking.

"Please follow me this way," he said.

"Sir, I swear I'm innocent. I haven't committed any crimes," she kept saying as they were leaving the building.

He asked her to get into the back of a sedan. A second man on the driver's seat was also wearing civilian clothes.

"Are you military?"

"No, Miss Castle, we are the police."

"What's happening? Where are you taking me?" She was still unsure if the men were telling the truth.

"This was an unfortunate case of a mistaken identity. I'm really sorry this happened to you. We're going to take you home now."

As they drove away, she noticed it was dark outside.

"What time is it, captain?"

"It's almost nine o'clock."

"You're telling me the truth, right? You're not gonna kill me."

"We're not assassins, Miss Castle. You're safe and we're taking you home." He then extended his hand. "Here. Your keys."

She remembered her truck was parked right outside Freddy's house.

"Captain, I work at Santa Maria Hospital. Is something going on there?"

"Why are you asking?"

"I overheard the guards talking about it."

"The Archbishop has been admitted there, so a lot of security and reporters and cameras are all over, but otherwise nothing unusual as far as I know."

"Captain, the people that brought me here…" she hesitated for a second… "They are not with the police, right?"

"They are not," Vidal said.

"They look like part of the military. How did you learn about me? Who told you to come and rescue me?"

Vidal did not reply.

"Captain Vidal, are those men part of the group known as the Frenchies?"

Vidal did not reply.

The Frenchies. The ruthless paramilitary group, probably supported by the government, had kidnapped her and somehow, she had survived. But now they were on their way to her hospital.

"Do you mind if rather than driving me home we go to pick up my car?"

82

The Stranger looked at his watch. It was nine-thirty p.m. At that exact time, he saw two of the critical care nurses leaving the unit after help was urgently requested from the night supervisor's office. A bizarre accident involving several automobiles had occurred a few blocks from the hospital, and the emergency room was overwhelmed with the number of cases. The police guards that had been a constant presence outside the unit were not there. The door of the ICU was not locked as usual. As he slowly walked in, there was a short entrance way where gowns were hanging from the wall and a table with boxes of surgical masks and disposable shoe covers. He did not see any security people around. The six patients were in a single open space with three beds situated at each side. Every bed was occupied by an intubated patient on a ventilator. The lighting was minimal, with the idea to maintain the natural awake–sleep cycle. Except for the constant beeps of the cardiac monitors, the room was extremely quiet. He saw a very young nurse in the back office updating the charts. He recognized her face. She had recently graduated and was probably inexperienced and naive and if needed, a brief *I'm doing a quick check for the attending on call* would probably suffice to get her out of his way. He looked at the numbers on top of the beds. 1-2-3-4-5. Number five. It was him. He recognized his face. He stood up next to the bed and looked at the old man for a few seconds. It was him. There was no doubt. Archbishop Villena-Alarcon was lying on an ICU bed. A white linen bed sheet covered the lower half of his body. He had a breathing tube coming out of his mouth. A central line catheter on the right internal jugular vein, an arterial catheter on his left wrist and a Foley urinary catheter. He was receiving morphine IV every few hours to keep him comfortable. Despite the precarious position that he was in, there was something dignifying about him.

"Good evening, Father" he said as he opened his fanny pack.

The patient in bed 5 slowly opened his eyes.

"Do you remember me, Father?"

The priest looked straight at the stranger's eyes.

"It's been so many years." He then put on his headphones and pressed play while grabbing a syringe from inside his fanny pack.

The priest's pupils rapidly increased in size and the heart monitor beeps almost doubled in frequency.

"There is no reason for so much pain."

83

Isabella's truck was still parked in the same place, about half a block from Freddy's house. It was crazy to think this was the same place she was just taken away from less than forty-eight hours ago.

She drove for a few blocks and then she parked next to a public phone booth. She placed a coin, dialed the house number and after a few rings, felt relieved to hear her Mother's voice on the other side.

"Mom, it's me!" she said, trying to contain her emotion.

"Isabella, my God! Are you okay?"

"Yes, Mom, I'm okay. I was detained by the military but it was a case of mistaken identity."

"Oh my God, those fucking idiots…" she started saying.

"Hey Mom, listen," Isabella interrupted. She was tired, hungry and dirty. There was nothing else that she wanted at that moment other than going home, taking a shower and going to bed. "I need to stop by the hospital really quickly and then I'll be on my way. Okay? I love you." And then she hung up.

As she turned the car engine on, the stereo system automatically started playing the last tape she had been listening to.

Right away, she recognized the guitar intro of the Pixies' "Where Is My Mind?"

Fuck.

84

Guillermo tried to do his best walking in between the tightly packed crowd of people while holding a glass of rum and coke. The music was loud and the heavy cigarette smoke in the air blurred the partygoers' faces, making the scene even more unreal.

"Guillermo! How are you doing, brother?" Mario said with a huge smile.

"I haven't had this much fun in a long time!"

Mario raised his beer "Cheers, brother!"

"You're very happy to see me a bit intoxicated, aren't you?"

"You bet I am."

"Who are all these people? I don't think I know half of them!"

"Many of them are friends from previous lives."

Guillermo moved his head rhythmically with the music. He knew it was a song by The Cars but he couldn't remember the name. "Good music," he said with his right thumb up.

"You need to keep alternating between pop, rock and salsa to keep everybody happy."

"Cheers for that!" He raised his glass.

"I saw you talking to Stella a bit ago. She's looking really hot tonight!"

Guillermo grabbed a little piece of paper from inside his pocket.

"What's that?"

"I got her phone number!"

"Fucking awesome, brother!"

Guillermo wanted to go back and talk to her again, maybe offer her a drink, when he saw Andrea.

"Hey Andrea, what's up?"

"It looks like you're having a great time!"

"Awesome party!"

"Isabella's Mom just called me to let me know that they found her and that she's okay."

"Oh my god, that's so awesome, it makes me feel so happy." He could feel his facial muscles getting sore from smiling nonstop.

And kind of out of nowhere he asked "Can I give you a hug?"

Andrea smiled. "Of course."

"And how come she is not here?"

"Her Mom said she needed to stop by the hospital first to pick up some stuff."

Not really used to drinking very much, a bit of scotch, rum and beer, suddenly he had the need to go outside to throw up.

"Excuse me, Andrea, I've got to go outside. I'll talk to you in a bit."

85

Driving to Santa Maria Hospital that night could not have been any more challenging. The main road had been closed without previous advice and the traffic was simply terrible. Isabella had to maneuver her way around the small side streets to finally get to the back of the hospital where the residents' and interns' parking lot was. She grabbed her ID tag and put on her white lab coat that was still in the car after all these days.

She ran to the ED first where everything looked absolutely chaotic, with a multitude of patients waiting to be seen, health care workers running around and the unusual presence of several police officers.

"What happened ?" she asked one of the nurses.

"There was a major accident a few blocks from here involving multiple cars and people. As you can see we're extremely busy, so you're more than welcome to help, there are multiple lacerations that need to be sutured."

"Okay, I need to check on something first. I'll be back."

Multiple victims in the ED; would it be a good place for the killer to attack next? Probably not due to the heavy police presence. But the guards talked about something happening at the hospital hours ago before the accident happened.

She then ran to the ICU, where she heard the Archbishop had been admitted and was critically ill. *With all this madness in the ED, nobody is paying attention to the ICU.*

She opened the door of the ICU, which would normally be locked from the inside and immediately saw two nurses doing chest compressions. One of the intensivists had just arrived after her and started yelling orders.

"How long have you been doing CPR for?"

"About five minutes," said one of the nurses.

"Go ahead and push one amp of epinephrine!"

Isabella got closer to the patient in bed 5 as the team continued the resuscitation efforts. He looked at the Archbishop's face and chest but could not see any marks.

"Hold compressions and check for a pulse now," he said.

"No pulse," said one of the nurses.

"Okay. Continue CPR."

Gradually more staff showed up to help.

Isabella instinctively grabbed the patient's hand, something she had seen before, when the staff had a feeling that the patient was going to die, maybe to let them know that they were not alone.

"The monitor shows v-fib."

"Okay guys, we are gonna shock, everybody's clear!"

Isabella let go of the priest's hand for a few seconds for the electric shock to be delivered, but when she grabbed the hand again she could clearly see the black cross in the base of the patient's thumb.

She stepped back slowly, looking down, knowing that she had failed to protect another patient. An overwhelming feeling of nausea appeared. Not knowing what to do for a second, she left the unit. She walked a few steps outside towards some bushes and tried to make herself throw up, but she couldn't. There was nothing in her stomach.

Then all of a sudden, she knew what to do.

86

"Having a good time?" It wasn't until Guillermo heard his voice that he realized Carlos was sitting next to him. He had just thrown up and was not feeling very stable on his feet.

"Hey Carlos, I didn't see you early. Did you just get here?"

Usually outgoing and cheerful, Carlos didn't look quite the same.

"I've been here for a while. Have you heard about Isabella?" There was something ominous about his voice.

"Actually, I have. She's okay. Andrea just told me. I don't know the details of what happened yet, but Andrea told me she's okay."

Carlos did not reply for a few minutes. He looked around. They were the only two people sitting outside on the patio. "It was Freddy," he said.

All of a sudden Guillermo did not feel drunk anymore. *Did he just say it was Freddy?*

"What?"

"I'm afraid Freddy has something to do with Isabella's disappearance. A few months ago, I saw him leaving one the wards right before they called a code blue. His attitude was kind of suspicious. When I asked him if he had something to do with that, he didn't deny it."

"I don't understand? Why?"

"He said somebody needed to do it. Freddy is a very strange person. I think something in his childhood really messed him up. He blames her Mother for his Dad's passing. I've been to his house. He reads a lot of weird books that somehow he interprets through music, some shit like that, that I don't even understand."

"How come you didn't say anything?"

Carlos looked down, like he was embarrassed. "I don't know. I was afraid, I guess." He also knew Isabella was asking questions around and looking into all these patients that mysteriously died at the hospital.

"Where is he now?"

"He said he had one more job to do. "

"You mean another killing?"

"I don't know. I think so."

"You mean he is in the hospital right now?"

Carlos nodded.

"Isabella is on her way to the hospital. She must know something and she's gonna try to stop him!"

"Sorry man, that means she's in danger."

"I need to go right now. Can I borrow your car?"

"No way, brother. You're too drunk to drive!"

87

Isabella opened the door of the residents' call room building. She stood there for a moment. She was afraid, but her heart was not racing and her hands were not shaking. The main lounge lights were off but she could see a light coming from the end of the hallway where the lockers were. She only needed to take a few steps to confirm that she was right.

"Hi, Freddy! Are you going somewhere?"

Freddy was in the process of emptying out his locker in a hurry. He turned around and appeared surprised for a few seconds, but then he smiled calmly.

"My dear Isabella, you are probably the smartest person I know."

"You just killed the Bishop, right?"

"Archbishop, to be precise. Not my choice, though. It was a job I was asked to do."

"Requested by whom?"

"It's better that you don't know."

She walked a few steps towards him. Close enough to look directly at his eyes.

"You killed Mrs. Jimenez. Why? She was my patient!" Thinking about it made her very angry.

"Mrs. Jimenez was one of the few survivors of the Barrios Altos massacre. A potential witness of the Frenchies' barbaric methods. They had to be sure she was not around to testify against them."

"Barbaric methods? What about you? You kill defenseless patients."

"I've been perfecting my technique for a few years now. They die mostly peacefully. There's nothing barbaric about it. It's actually more like an art."

"You're a sick man, Freddy."

"You got to give me some credit. I'm really good at what I do." His tone was not restrained as usual but rather there was something devilish about it.

"I'm not sure about that. Since the place was under full surveillance, that only means that you had help from the inside. Someone from the military or the government is helping you."

"You're so fucking smart."

"But they cannot keep you around. You are a precious witness, so they will either kill you too or send you far away."

"I guess it's time to say goodbye, Isabella. I noticed something special about you since the first time I saw you in med school. Too bad we won't get to be together again."

He pulled another syringe from his fanny pack, and slowly walked towards her.

"I always keep an extra one ready in case of problems."

Isabella just realized she made a big mistake coming alone to the hospital.

"My dear Isabella, you don't know how much I admire you," he said as his left hand grabbed her by the throat, pushing her violently against the wall.

Isabella could barely move. She focused on taking slow deep breaths to keep her oxygen levels normal to avoid passing out. Everything started to get blurry when her peripheral vision detected Freddy's right hand holding a syringe slowly getting closer to her neck. Without thinking, her right hand reached inside her lab coat pocket where she had left the disposable red scalpel.

Freddy lent forward and kissed her forehead. For a fraction of second, he decreased the strength of the hold around her neck when the scalpel stabbed his left shoulder with fury.

He jumped back instinctively, screaming in pain. He looked surprised seeing the sleeve of his shirt filling up with blood quickly.

"Fuck! What did you just do?" Now his eyes were staring at her in anger.

He was getting ready to charge again when a voice came from nowhere.

"Enough Freddy!"

Freddy hesitated for a second.

"Enough, I said. We have to go. I have a car waiting."

It was Cazorla.

Isabella's eyes widened. She was right to think the Dean had been involved.

"And you, Isabella, don't tell anyone what you just saw. Military intelligence knows who you are and they will look for you and they will make you disappear if you ever tell anything to anyone."

Freddy looked at her. Unexpectedly his eyes appeared sad.

"I wasn't really gonna hurt you. I guess it's time to go. Bye Isabella. We'll see each other again. I promise."

88

Casals had stopped the ED first and later in the ICU where the team of doctors and nurses had finally stopped resuscitative efforts unable to bring the Archbishop back. He could not find Isabella. Guillermo had told him to also check in the call room.

He opened the door and turned the lights on.

He found Isabella sitting on the floor probably unable to move from the overwhelming mix of emotions. Without saying anything, Casals sat next to her.

It felt like an eternity before she found her voice.

"It was Freddy who killed those patients."

"I know. I spoke with Cazorla. He told me everything"

"Why?"

"Freddy had a difficult childhood. He blames his Mother for his Dad's suicide. Dr. Cazorla tried to help him all along. When Freddy started his clinical rotations is when he started experimenting how to induce cardiac arrest in the most effective way. Not only Cazorla found out but also military intelligence. General Montero has spies everywhere. They had a deal where they would not charge him for the murders as long as he did occasional inside jobs for them when needed."

"And the Archbishop?"

"The Archbishop was very critical of the government. Peru is almost entirely Catholic, and the church's opinion matters. I imagine they needed a friendlier clergy."

She shook her head in disbelief.

"Do you believe in God, Dr. Casals?"

Casals looked for the most appropriate answer. It didn't take him too long to find it.

"My Dad died five years ago. He was a very intelligent man. Never attended college but was very knowledgeable about everything. He owned over a hundred books in his library and I know for sure he read them all. I loved talking to him. It was hard to see his cognitive abilities slowly deteriorate because of Alzheimer's. I miss him so much. Sometimes I found myself talking to him. And as incredible as it may sound, I can feel his presence. I know it's not possible from a physical standpoint but still, I will talk to him. Because maybe, somehow, I want to believe he is still among us."

He looked around the empty room and then got up slowly.

"It's time we go home."

89

Isabella didn't go to work the next day. She slept in her bed until past noon.

Her Mother brought her breakfast to bed.

She called Andrea and let her know that everything was okay.

But she was mostly hoping to have an honest talk with her Father. He came back home earlier than usual. Mr. Castle knocked her door gently and then walked into her room slowly and sat in the bed, next to her.

"Hi baby," he said.

"Hi Dad."

"Are you okay?"

"I feel better."

"Your Mom and I were so worried."

"That's okay. I'm home now." She hesitated for a few seconds, afraid to bring the topic up "Dad, I need to ask you something. It's about my brother. Do you hate Diego?"

He looked surprised. "Of course not, baby. I love your brother."

"But didn't he leave because of you? He is gay and he knew that you didn't approve of it, and that's why he left, right?

"No, that's not how it happened. Of course, I know he is gay. We talked about it many times. We talked about whether it was better for his future to move to the United States. It was his decision at the end that I supported. I love him the way he is and I want him to be happy."

"Thank you," she said, and then she hugged him like she hadn't done in a long time.

90

The first person that Isabella saw when she walked in the medical ward the next morning was Nurse Carol.

"How are you, Doctor Castle? We were very worried about you."

"I'm okay. Thank you, Miss Carol." She actually felt relieved to see that old charge nurse looking well. "I'm happy to be back."

"Hey Isabella," a familiar voice behind her said. It was Guillermo.

"Hi! How are things here?"

"It's all good."

"How are you?"

"I'm doing well, thank you for asking."

"A case of mistaken identity! Really? Is that what they say? That's such bullshit! You could have died."

"I'm just happy to be back at work."

"Did you hear the news?"

"No. Something happened?"

"Cazorla died. He was found dead sitting at his desk in his office. Very weird."

She took a deep breath and then she said, "Cardiac event maybe?"

"Who knows?"

"Hey, how was the party? I heard that you have a girlfriend now."

"Who? Stella? Oh, not at all. I called her a couple of times but I don't think she is very interested in going out with me."

"Well, there will be many other girls in the future, I can assure you."

He shrugged.

"Sorry if you had to work harder in my absence."

"No worries. Actually, we had a young patient that we diagnosed with a new acute leukemia. We tried to transfer him to the National Cancer Institute but they didn't have beds, so while waiting, we got him started on a full chemotherapy regimen with a very good response. Very exciting case. So now I'm seriously thinking in doing an Oncology specialty."

"I heard the National Cancer Institute program is very good."

"That's right. So I'm looking into it. I may not have to leave the country."

91

The old Restaurant Cordano, located only a couple of blocks from Congress, is a favorite place for politicians and legislators to have lunch and socialize after work. It was also the preferred place for Captain Vidal to have an early dinner every time his busy job would allow it.

He had already ordered a *lomo saltado*, enjoyed the first sip of the classic Peruvian cocktail known as *pisco sour* and quietly started reading the newspaper when a man stood up next to his table.

"Do you mind if I sit down?"

He looked up and recognized the tall, dark figure in front of him.

"Of course not, captain Rincon. Please have a seat."

"I'm going to be brief. The general is upset about what you did."

"You know that order came directly from God's representative on earth."

"We're well aware. And that's the only reason why you are still here enjoying a good lunch."

Vidal sipped on his drink one more time without avoiding eye contact.

"So, I just wanted to let you know that if you ever make a move against us again, it will be your last time."

Vidal nodded in silence while looking into the eyes of who he knew was the leader of the Frenchies. Then he pointed at his glass.

"You know what? This is a really good Pisco Sour."

92

Casals opened the door to let the last patient of the day come in. It had been a busy day in the clinic and he was ready to go home. He was caught by surprise when he saw the familiar face.

"Good afternoon, Dr. Casals!"

"Father Silvestri! Such an unexpected visit!" For a second, he didn't know what to say. The Bishop looked taller and certainly more imposing in person.

"Please come in. Have a seat. How can I help you?"

Silvestri looked around the modest office with no pictures or diplomas on the walls.

"You see, I was seeing a general practitioner in Ayacucho but since I've been relocated back to the capital, I'm gonna need a new doctor."

"Relocated? I'd say promoted."

"Thank you. Your old friend Cazorla always spoke very highly of you. Before he passed, of course. Such a sad event. But anyway, I've been having pain and swelling on my right big toe for a while now and he thought it could be gout, and he told me that you would be somebody with a good knowledge of internal medicine and rheumatologic conditions."

"Well, that was very nice of him. Do you want to tell me more about these complaints? For how long have you had them?" Casals asked as he grabbed a pen and opened the chart.

"Before we go into my medical stuff, let me ask you something." Silvestri sat back on the chair and crossed his right leg over. "I think doctors are like priests in a way. Would you agree? We both are fully dedicated to our jobs and have a spiritual connection to our professions. Doctors are also like priests in the sense that everything the patient tells them is to remain a secret, correct? Just like in a Confession."

"That is correct, Father, doctors have to honor the patient's rights for privacy and confidentiality."

"You are a smart man, Dr. Casals, and I feel like you need an explanation of what happened surrounding the death of the Archbishop Villena- Alarcon."

"You don't really need to tell me anything."

"I think I do. The real reason the Archbishop is not with us anymore is not because I wanted to take his position or because Opus Dei wanted to be in control of our church or because it's strategic for the government to have an ally like me instead, in the war against terrorism. That's what the government and military intelligence believe. But it's not entirely true."

Casals put the pen down. Silvestri had his full attention.

"The real reason is because Villena-Alarcon liked boys."

Astonished by this answer, it took a few seconds for Casals to react. "Excuse me, Father? What did you just say?"

"Our Archbishop liked young boys so much that he could not stop himself."

"Did you say boys? How many are we talking about?"

"Many cases over many years. More than twenty for sure. Nobody knows exactly. Unfortunately, the Archbishop had become too dangerous for our church. An enormous liability for the entire Catholic world and we ran out of options. He had been approached by some of the church leaders and even by myself personally. He was asked about leaving his post. He was offered a very good retirement package. Even the Vatican offered him the chance to be relocated to Rome but he declined the idea."

"So, you partnered with the military to get rid of him but they don't know the real reason."

"Cazorla was right. You are a very smart man, Dr. Casals."

"Did the Pope approve your plan?"

"We have complete freedom in how to manage all our local businesses." He smiled.

"Why are you telling me all this, Father?"

"Don't you see, Dr. Casals? As my doctor now, all this information is safe with you. The government and The Doc won't have to worry about you. Too many people have died already."

"I don't understand." He hesitated for a second and suddenly he knew.

"Yes, you do. Now that you are my doctor, you won't be able to tell anything to anybody. Patient confidentiality just like in the Sacrament of Confession. The secret stays with you."

"You're safe now. That's it. Now let me tell you about this arthritis that is becoming such a pain in my butt."

93

It was early December and the slightly warm weather was a little reminder that summer was right around the corner.

At first, Andrea did not recognize her.

"Hey stranger, how have you been?"

"Hi there!" Isabella was happy to see her friend again since... when was the last time they saw each other? A couple of months?

"Look at you! Your hair is getting so long, it looks good."

"Thank you."

"And you look much more relaxed."

"I am. I'm really enjoying my elective rotation on infectious diseases. And I don't have to take calls. What rotation are you on?"

"I'm doing medicine with Casals. You already know how it is, busy, busy, busy!"

Andrea looked at her friend's clothes. Underneath her white coat, Isabella was wearing a light blue shirt, dark blue jeans and white sneakers.

"No more dark outfits, ah? Don't you have to show how tough you are?"

Isabella smiled and shook her head. "I guess not anymore."

"Remember that song that we listened to in your house that we both like so much?"

"Yeah, I remember. 'Pure' by the Lightning Seeds."

"Yes. A friend of mine that works at a radio station found this acoustic version," Andrea said as she gave her friend a cassette tape with her name. "It's the first song in the A side."

"Oh, thank you. You're so sweet."

"When you go home today, I want you to play it in the car. Okay?"

"I definitely will."

"I have to get back to the unit. I have a new admit coming from the ER."

"See you later then. I'm finishing earlier today. Maybe I'll try to go to the gym. It's been a while."

By the time Isabella left it was early afternoon and it was still sunny and warm outside. As she walked towards the parking lot she realized she was smiling. She had not felt this good in a long time. She got into her car, turned the engine on and could not wait to listen to the tape that Andrea gave her a few moments earlier. As the cassette started playing she did not recognize the song. *That's not the Lightning*

Seeds. It was a weird song that she had never heard before. She listened to the lyrics with attention.

> *I am he as you are he as you are me*
>
> *And we are all together*
>
> *See how they run like pigs from a gun*
>
> *See how they fly*
>
> *I'm crying*
>
> *I am the egg man*
>
> *They are the egg man*
>
> *I am the walrus.*

Father Juan Carlos Silvestri was named Cardinal in 1998 by Pope John Paul II.

He was the first Opus Dei priest to be made Cardinal.

After Pope John Paul II passed away, Cardinal Ratzinger was elected Pope in 2005.

He adopted the name of Benedict XVI. He resigned from the papacy in 2013 allegedly due to health problems.